The Warrior's
Wounds

Book Four of the McGinn
Family Saga
J.E. McCarthy

West Front Media, LLC

This book is dedicated to my grandfather Roy Gallant, my uncle Wilfred Dubois and all of my other relatives of that generation that sacrificed so much for their country.

INTRODUCTION

I don't typically do an introduction with my books, but I feel like this one requires one. This book spans the time of World War Two, both at home and abroad. The portions that deal with the war are realistic to the best of my research. I highly recommend the book Into the Rising Sun, by Patrick K O'Donnell. It is comprised of firsthand accounts by veterans of the Pacific theater. The stories were so profound that they sometimes brought me to tears and made me wish that I could go back to my relatives that have long passed away and show them my respect for their courage and sacrifice.

This book is graphic in both violence and language at times, but not gratuitous and I feel like any *sugar coating* of this subject would be a disgrace to those who served so valiantly.

One

December 1941

Patrick was up early and washed before chow. They had been in dock for a while and weekends were great for seeing Oahu. It was Saturday morning, and he was going to tour part of the island with some guys from the aft torpedo room.

Their cruise had been uneventful, and they were in Pearl for a general overhaul. Patrick was enjoying shore life, but he liked being under the sea rather than on top of it. When the boat was surfaced, he was vulnerable.

He had spent the early hours of Saturday calculating the hours between Hawaii and Maine. He was counting down his sister's marriage back home. He had strolled around base waiting until a few minutes before 10AM and he found the first open bar and ordered a shot of whiskey. It would be 4PM in Maine and he calculated that's when the toasts might be going around. In his mind, he could picture Ruth and Joe. Ruth in

1

a white gown that Emma would have made and Joe in a black tuxedo, looking like a grinning fool. He liked Joe a lot and was happy Ruth had agreed to marry him. Joe was roughly the same age as Jim would have been, and he had red hair as well. Obviously, he would never be Jim, but he considered him another brother. His brother-in-law Bill was a great guy, but he wasn't like the McGinns. He had never known any real hardship. Joe grew up poor, like the McGinns, so the fit seemed natural.

About a minute before ten, he grabbed the shot of Irish Whiskey and started counting down. He stared at the brown liquor in the glass and smiled.

The bartender looked at him with a frown. "Hey buddy, the glasses are clean here."

"I know. I'm waiting."

The bartender stopped what he was doing. "For what?"

"For my family to toast my sister and her new husband."

The bartender nodded, smiled and poured a shot for himself. "What time is it back home?"

"Nearly four in the afternoon. It's in Maine."

"Holy shit," said the bartender. "I think you might be on the exact opposite spot on the earth from Maine."

Patrick chuckled, "It sure feels that way."

The bartender looked at the clock. "Thirty seconds?"

"Yes sir. That's what I have."

The bartender poured himself a shot. "I don't want you to drink alone."

Patrick smiled from ear to ear. "Five, four, three, two, one...Slainte M'hath."

"And to your health too... McGinn," as he read the name on Patrick's uniform.

They had their shots and Patrick decided to try to have something to eat.

"Are you serving still breakfast?" asked Patrick.

The bartender shook his head. "No, but I could serve you a sandwich if you'd like."

Patrick perked up. "Hey, can you make a Club Sandwich?"

"Yeah. Of course, I can. Is that what you want?"

"Yes please. And a black coffee."

"No more whiskey?"

Patrick shook his head. "No, I'm not really much of a drinker. But I know what my family would be doing, and I wanted to be a part of it."

"Fair enough. A club and a coffee coming up."

After lunch, he walked around the city. It was swarming with sailors and marines. The crowds made him nervous. Too many men, too much liquor and too few women. He used to think an attractive woman in town, would have a parade of sailors chasing her around. At first, he thought she might be flattered, but he suspected that after a while, it would grow old. And as if on cue, a sailor strode forward with a woman on his arm. She was a small beauty with strawberry blonde hair and big blue eyes. To Patrick, she looked a lot like his sister-in-law Daisy, and it made him feel a little homesick. But his moment of nostalgia was broken by a big Marine who was walking toward the couple with a menacing scowl.

"What the hell Becky?!" he bellowed, and the conversations on the street went silent.

"I can see who I want, Gene," she replied and started to pass him by. He reached out and snatched her free arm.

"Ow, you're hurting me," she protested, and her date stepped in. He was all of one-hundred and fifty pounds soaking wet. The Marine had him by six inches and sixty pounds, by Patrick's best guess.

Her cry made every man in the immediate vicinity stand up and decide they would make a good hero to the maiden fair as well.

Her date stepped up to the Marine with an authoritative posture. "Take your hands off from her sailor," he said.

He let go and faced her date, looming over him. "I'm a Marine, not a sailor. Sailor"

"Well, I'm an Ensign, not a sailor."

The big Marine leaned in a little closer. "Am I supposed to be impressed?"

The Ensign chuckled. "Well, I was rather hoping that she would be impressed," he said, jerking his thumb toward his date.

Becky pulled out of his grip, rubbing her arm. "I'm not some piece of meat to be fought over by a pack of hungry dogs." She turned to the Marine with her fists on her hips. "Eugene. We went on one date and that's as many as you were ever going to get. You're boorish when you start drinking, your breath is foul, and you kiss like a cow chewing cud." The sailors and marines in the crowd roared with laughter. "Girls like a kiss that is firm, but gentle." She looked at the Ensign and shook her head, her eyes fixed on Patrick, and she grabbed him by the navy-blue knot on his neckerchief and pulled his face to hers and kissed him.

Patrick could feel his face burn as he blushed, but he realized the ribbing he'd suffer if he looked like a scared kid. So, he relaxed and kissed her gently back. The laughter changed to hoots and whistles. They kissed for about ten seconds, but it seemed like an eternity, and he didn't want to stop.

She released his knot and slowly stopped the kiss and smiled at him, continuing to stare into his eyes. "Now, that's how a girl likes to be kissed and his breath tastes of whiskey." Patrick blushed again. "I like a small drop of whiskey every now and then."

"I have whiskey breath!" someone called from the crowd. "Yeah, me too!" called another. This started another chorus of laughter.

"Can you walk me home?" she said to Patrick.

"Me?" he said, feeling a little confused.

"Yes you. No funny business, just a walk."

"Oh, yes, Ma'am."

"Ma'am? How formal." She held her hand out, and he gave her his left elbow. They walked past the Marine and the Ensign and neither said a word. They stood in stunned silence. Becky never gave them a glance and Patrick shrugged as he walked by.

"Where would you like me to take you...Miss?"

"Oh, let's move out of sight of those clowns and I'll take myself from there. Rebecca Crowley is my name. But please call me Becky."

"I'm Patrick McGinn and pleased to meet you."

She glanced back over her shoulder and be certain they weren't being followed. "Okay, Mr. McGinn. Thank you for your services. I'm going here."

Patrick looked up at the looming white facade of the base hospital. "Do you work here?"

"I do. I am a nurse."

"Oh wow! My sister-in-law back in Maine is a nurse."

"Well, that makes your brother a very lucky man. Being married to a nurse keeps you healthy."

Patrick cocked his head sideways in bewilderment. "How?"

"Cleanliness. We like things to be sterile, so a nurse's husband is less likely to be sick," she said with a smile.

"Oh, I never thought of it that way, I guess."

She laughed out loud. "You're so serious. There's no proof of that, but men do feel safer around nurses. My patients tell me far more than I would ever want to know."

Patrick smiled as she was laughing. She had a beautiful smile. "Becky, it has been nice meeting you. I need to head back to the boat."

"Maybe I'll see you at church in the morning." She said, studying his face.

"Oh ah, I'll probably be there, but it's the Catholic mass."

"I know. I've seen you at mass before."

Patrick blushed and felt embarrassed he didn't recognize her. "I'm sorry Becky. I don't recall seeing you at church."

"Well, I've seen you and I expect you to be in church tomorrow. Play your cards right, and we'll have a picnic lunch near the airfield, and you can tell me all about your boat."

Patrick smiled from ear to ear. "I would like that very much!"

"Okay. I'll see you at church then. I like to go to the early Mass. It's not as crowded."

Patrick nodded in agreement. "Oh, me too. I'm an early riser. Tomorow then."

They parted, and he headed back to the boat. As he walked up the gangplank, the crew on deck started whistling and laughing.

"What's so funny?" he asked with a scowl.

Riggs was a torpedoman in the forward room and liked to prank guys on the boat. "Red is a great color on you, McGinn. Don't get it on your uniform. It's hard to wash out, Loverboy."

"McGinn!" yelled a voice. It was the gravelly growl of Chief Petty Officer Halpert.

"Yes, Chief!" He replied instinctively.

"Wipe that god damned lipstick off from your mouth."

Patrick pulled a signal mirror from his pocket and looked at his face. The lipstick was bright red. The exact bright red Becky had been wearing. "Oh, that little sneak." He said aloud. He must have looked proper fool walking by the men after he got kissed. At first, he was a little embarrassed, but then he thought, *the hell with it. Let em' wonder I'm the one that she chose.*

He wiped his mouth and as quickly as the ribbing began; the men were back about the mechanical business of tending the boat.

The next morning, Patrick was up and out of bed early. He had put on his best sailor's whites and headed for the deck. As he grabbed the ladder to the surface, the whole boat shook, and everyone heard what sounded like an explosion. Since the sub was in for repairs, they only had a skeleton crew to maintain her while refitting was being done. Then the boat shook again and again. Patrick shot for the surface as quickly as he could. When he emerged from below, the sky was filled with planes and the air was thick with screams and smoke.

He stood there trying to comprehend what he was seeing, when he heard Halpert call his name again. "McGinn! Get to that forward deck gun and shoot any plane that comes in range."

Patrick grabbed a helmet and flak jacket from a locker inside the sub and ran to the forward gun. He loaded a shell and slammed the breech home with a loud click. He looked around for help and tried to aim the gun himself. The air was filled with tracer rounds and smoke and when he saw a plane coming into range, he fired the big guns. Flame licked from the barrel, and he thought that he had hit a plane, but with so much firing, there was no way to know for sure and he really couldn't understand why it was bothering him that he might not get credit for a kill.

Three more men emerged from below deck and ran to assist.

"Mac! What do you need for help?" Riggs screamed trying to make himself heard over the din of war.

"Just keep my ammo coming!" he replied.

Two men mounted the gun to help aim and they kept up steady fire. Patrick could distinctly hear the sound of a torpedo plane beginning to dive, but it was so smokey that he couldn't always pick targets until they were right on top of them. "Torpedo plane somewhere! Find it!" he called and Riggs, started scanning the skies.

"Holy shit! Ten O' clock Mac! Ten O' clock!"

Patrick swung the gun around and unloaded on the plane. The cockpit widow exploded, and the plane began to roll off from its dive and into one of the few spaces in the harbor not occupied by naval vessels.

"Great job Mac!" yelled Riggs.

"Keep spotting!"

"I want to fire the gun!" he replied. Patrick thought for a moment and then relented.

"Okay Riggs. I'll spot for you!"

Just as they changed places, the deck boards began to explode in gunfire and slivers of wood were flying everywhere. The barrel of the gun came swinging around and knocked him to the deck. He felt a burning on his right forearm with followed by a sickening hiss as the red-hot barrel burned his arm.

"Shit Riggs! Watch the barrel!" He shouted and when he got up from the deck, Riggs was as pale as a ghost and blood was pouring from his neck. Patrick jumped to help his shipmate and Riggs collapsed. There were holes in his chest and abdomen as well. He checked for a pulse, but Riggs was already dead. Patrick hauled his body out of the way and returned to his firing position. He searched the sky, and his forearm was pounding with pain. He saw another fighter coming in for a strafing run, and he made himself compact and fired. He led the plane a little and then a little more. He thought the round had hit home, but the plane pulled off from its attack and didn't explode.

"Come back here you god damned cowards!"

A moment later, he was flying as if in a dream and everything went dark.

Two

Sunday dinners had become much smaller in recent years. The older children all came when they could, but tonight it would just be the ones who still lived at home. It was the day after Ruth and Joe's wedding, and everyone was worn out from the festivities.

Ruth and Joe had gone to Watertown for their honeymoon, to stay in a hotel and see the city. It had been mild for the wedding, but today it was starting to feel like winter in Maine. The wind had stiffened out of the north, and everything felt ten degrees colder than it should have.

Sean was adding wood to the stove when he saw Alder's truck come flying into the driveway skidding to a stop. "Ma. Alder is here," he said. "He looks to be in a hurry."

Mary saw someone run across the yard and bound up the steps for the front door. Alder flung the door open out of breath. "Turn on the radio! Japan attacked Hawaii!"

Mary felt the blood drain from her body, and she felt weak for a moment. "Patrick," she whispered.

Alder started tuning the radio until he could get a clear sounding station. Everyone crowded around the table-top *Philco* radio in desperate anticipation.

"Sean, go to the barn and get Alston and tell him to get in here."

"I will Ma!" and a second later he was out the door.

Alder caught his breath up. "Japan attacked Pearl Harbor early in the morning and there were a lot of ships destroyed and men killed."

"Oh no. Was Pat's submarine hit?" asked Lillian.

Alder shook his head. "We haven't heard anything about submarines, but a bunch of battleships were hit and some sunk."

The Philco crackled and snapped until suddenly a clear voice emerged. "*We don't have official numbers as of yet, but initial reports say more than two-thousand dead and another one-thousand wounded. Multiple ships sunk, including two battleships and several destroyers.*"

"Two thousand," said Frances. Her eyes were wide as she tried to think if she had known two-thousand people in her entire life.

Alston and Sean came crashing through the door, out of breath. "How bad is it?" said Alston, gasping for breath.

"Bad," replied Alder. "We haven't declared war yet, but they say it's inevitable."

Alston nodded in agreement. "Have they said what ships were hit?"

"No. Battle ships and Destroyers is what they have said so far."

Mary stood up. "Your brother is alive, and I don't want anyone to wonder about it. He's alive."

No one argued with her, and maybe she had a point. If they believed that he was safe, then it might make the *not knowing* that much easier to take.

The phone rang, and Frances ran to answer it. "McGinn residence." She paused and said, "Oh hi Finn, yes, we heard. It is so awful. So many dead." She listened some more, then turned to Mary. "Ma, do you want them to come over?"

Mary forced a smile. "Of course. I always want all of my children here."

"Yes, come over."

They all sat together for the next five hours and listened for any news of any kind. The reports kept coming in and there was no mention of the Narwhal. As the hour grew late, Frances, Sean and Lillian went to bed and only Mary and the boys remained awake.

Finn stood up. "I'm going to have a smoke and head out. Anyone care to join me?"

Everyone stepped into the summer kitchen to get out of the December night air.

Alder lit a pipe, and Finn smoked a cigarette. He offered one to Alston, but he declined. His mind was on Pat.

"I guess they'll be drafting a lot more guys soon," said Finn.

"They could draft all of us except Sean and, if it drags on at all, possibly him," said Alder.

Alston seemed puzzled. "But you and Lewin have families. Doesn't that count for something?"

"Hell no," said Finn. "If that was the case, guys would be running out, getting married and knocking up any woman they could get to say yes."

Mary reached out and took Alder's pipe. She put it to her lips and took a long drag. The embers blazed in the bowl of the pipe and Mary exhaled. "Back in the great war, all three of Maggie Murphy's sons were killed. The government doesn't care. We're nothing to them. Three neatly folded flags and no one left to hold or see married and live their lives. Only flags to look at. That's no trade at all for a mother."

Finn rubbed her shoulder. "We have to do our duty, Ma."

Mary shook her head. "Jesus. You sound like your father with all of his damned oaths of duty."

"Maybe we should enlist like Pat, so that we won't be in the infantry," said Alston.

Mary glared at him, and she saw his face. Her anger melted away. "You boys will do what you want. I know that. But we need to see what the next few days bring before you volunteer to run off to slaughter."

The next morning, the United States declared war on Japan, three days after that Germany. There was no going back. Everything they knew in life was going to be different.

Men were enlisting by thousands all across Maine. Alder had originally planned to wait to be drafted as did Lewin, but the pressure of seeing so many men enlist left them feeling like they were failing their country. They had talked about the needs of the family and the farms coming first, but their reasoning rang hollow and headed to the induction station with the others.

The car was stuffy with all five men piled in and Finn kept smoking cigarettes, making the men in the back nauseous.

"For Christ's sake Finn. Roll the window down and blow it out there," pleaded Lewin. "Joe and Alston don't even smoke."

"It helps me relax," he replied, "plus we'll all get pneumonia from a draft if the window is down."

Alston coughed. "If we don't die of suffocation first."

"Fine. I'll put it out." Finn tossed the butt out the window and rolled it up.

"Thank you," said Lewin.

They rode without speaking for a few minutes. Every man was contemplating their future. Except for Alston, they all had wives, and Alder and Lewin had children as well. They thought about saying goodbye to their loved ones. They thought about what might happen if they never came home. Most of all, they thought about what it would be like to look down the sights of a weapon and kill another man. They had all hunted, but those were animals. These are men. Men with wives and children and siblings and fathers and mothers, just like them. Mothers who would melt in despair reading the telegram that said they were dead and mothers that would hug a folded flag as it they were somehow touching their son one last time.

Alder broke the silence. "What are you guys thinking? What branch? Army or Navy?"

"Navy probably," said Alston. "Pat likes it." That was no surprise. They may have been born eleven months apart, but they were as close as any twins. "But who knows. Army maybe. I'm not good on boats."

"Lew?" asked Alder.

"I don't care. I'm thinking Army. I'm not much of a boat man. I'd be too seasick." Lewin participated, but he was far away in his mind. He was thinking of Cecelia and his children.

"Joe?"

He didn't hesitate. His brother John was a Marine, so that would be the best place for him as well. "Marines probably, John said they're some tough SOBs, and I'd fit right in. In fact, I'd say Finn was born for it."

"Finn?"

"The hell if I know. I'll go wherever they send me. They must know where they need guys the most." He reached into his pocket for his cigarettes and Lewin cleared his throat loudly, "Ahem".

Finn put the pack away. "Sorry. Habit. Alder, what about you? What do you want?"

"I don't care, just as long as I get home to my wife and girls."

Lewin reached forward and squeezed Alder's shoulder and nodded, fighting back some tears.

"Amen," said Joe. "We all need to come home. In one piece."

When they reached armory in Watertown, the line of men enlisting stretched around the corner. There must have been more than one-hundred men in line.

"Holy smokes. We're going to be here all day," said Alston.

"Well then. It's a good thing you tended the animals early, isn't it?" replied Finn.

Alston sighed and peered out the window. "They're going to be in rough shape, you know?"

"Who's that?" asked Alder.

"Ma, your wives. Sean is getting better at running the farm, but it's more than a one-man job," said Lewin. That thought added weight to their already heavy hearts.

Alder turned toward the back seat and gave him a father's look. "They are all tough and there are people around to help out. Frances and Lillian are both hard workers. I'm sure they'll be fine."

They spent the day speaking to recruiters and being poked and prodded by doctors, who were looking to see if they were fit to go kill other men. That was like the silliest part of the whole operation. They felt like as long as you could pull a trigger, you should be considered qualified.

They herded the men through alphabetically and Joe was separated from the McGinns. He was standing in line waiting for one of the Marine recruiters and was making small talk with the guy in front of him when a man in a navy-blue suit tapped him on the shoulder.

"Pardon me. I couldn't help but notice that you have a hint of an accent. Do you speak French by chance?"

Joe smiled. "I do. I have my whole life. I speak English outside of my home, but our whole family speaks French at home."

The man eyed him over carefully. Joe was an average height, but he was very muscular, and he stood out as someone who was likely very strong. The man asked quietly, "What do you do for work?"

Joe grinned. "I work in the woods as a lumberjack."

The man smiled and glanced about, as if looking for an escape. "Listen. These recruiters will still be here later today. Would you be willing to have a chat in private? It's a matter of national security and I can't say anything here."

"Sure. Lead the way." Said Joe and he followed the man into a conference room with two men and a woman seated at a large table. *This might be interesting*, he thought

"Have a seat," said the man in the navy suit and took a seat with the two men and the woman on the other side of the table. The chair that Joe was sitting in was a good three feet from the table, and it made Joe feel a little self-conscious. They were studying him, he realized, and now he felt really self -conscious.

They were not speaking, and the woman and one of the men were taking notes. The room was unusually dim because every shade was pulled. Finally, the woman stopped writing and studied Joe sitting in his chair, then said matter-of-factly, "*Mourriez-vous pour votre pays ?*"

Joe sat up straight and thought for a moment and smiled. "I think that I would rather kill for my country than die for it."

Three

Patrick's whole body ached, and he couldn't get the smell of gasoline and burned clothing out of his nostrils. He wiggled his fingers and toes and realized that he was, in fact, alive, but his left shoulder and left thigh were killing him. It took what felt like a great amount of exertion to open his eyes, and when he did, he realized that his vision had been partially obscured by a bandage. He reached up to move the bandage and heard a woman's voice.

"Don't touch that. You'll start it bleeding again."

"Becky?"

"Yes. I never made it to church."

Patrick groaned. "Me either. Is it over?"

"We don't know yet. I hope so."

He tilted his head so that he could see the room. Becky was wearing surgical clothes and her apron was covered in blood. It reminded him of the butcher Patrick and Alston had watched carve up hogs, back in Palmyra. In fact, the whole room smelled like blood, and he wasn't sure which was worse. His headache or the nausea he felt from the scent of blood.

He sniffed in vain, trying to get the blood and gasoline smells out of his nose, and then caught the acrid scent of burned hair. He winced as he reached up and touched his hair. It felt like someone had just cut it, but he realized that it was singed away. It was the same with the hair on his arms; they had an odd stubbly feeling to them.

"Becky, am I burnt bad?" he asked.

"No Pat. Just your hair and eyebrows in the front. But they'll grow back. It's like a bad sunburn. And of course, your arm was burned, but that will heal with some salve."

He tried to imagine what he'd look like, and the thought made him shudder. No eyebrows would be weird. He thought about the nicknames he'd get on the boat. *Damn, this will be a long cruise,* he thought.

She took his hand and squeezed it. "Don't worry. Your lips are intact."

He felt a flood of happiness for a quick second until his mind was ripped back to the carnage. He tilted his head to see her face beneath his bandage. "Are there many men killed or wounded?"

"Thousands," she whispered in a breaking voice, and he saw the tears forming in her eyes. He squeezed her hand back and tried to fight the tears himself. He released his grip and turned his face away.

"I'll check on you later. We have so many men to tend to."

He nodded silently and sniffled as the tears started pouring from his eyes. He thought about Riggs and started to wonder about Chief Halpert. The last he saw of him, Halpert was on the forward deck gun, but once the action started, the rest was a blur. His mind was dragged to the lifeless Riggs and his wide dead eyes and all the blood. He had a wife somewhere in upstate New York he remembered and started to weep as he thought of his wife hearing the news.

Why did this happen? He thought and drifted back to sleep.

When he opened his eyes again, he was on the farm and Alston was calling for him to come help with the milking. Alston was wearing an Army uniform, and Patrick was trying to understand why he was dressed that way.

Alston looked at him with his hands on his hips. "Pat, give me hand, will ya? Wake up."

When Patrick woke, he realized that he had been dreaming and tried to get his bearings. His forearm hurt terribly, and he remembered the hot gun barrel searing his flesh. When he peeked out from under the bandage, he expected to see Becky, but instead it was Chief Halpert sitting asleep in the chair beside the bed.

"Chief?" asked Patrick, not knowing if he was awake or still dreaming.

The Chief opened one eye and studied Patrick. "Christ McGinn, you were goofy looking enough with your red hair, but now you don't even have that."

At first, he felt a pang of anger at the humiliation, but then he realized that he was probably going to be alright. The chief would never say anything like that if he were going to die.

"Is the boat okay, chief?" he asked in a hoarse whisper.

Halpert turned the chair and faced Patrick. "Yeah. She's fine kid. Riggs is dead and a few guys who were on shore leave. The cook, Corson, was wounded but he'll live too."

"How about the rest of the fleet?"

"Pounded to shit. The Arizona sank with over a thousand men aboard."

"A thousand men?" Patrick's heart sunk. That was more than the whole population of Palmyra, killed in a single attack.

"The captain is recommending you for a commendation," said Halpert.

"A commendation? For what?"

"For shooting down a Jap plane and I imagine you'll get a Purple Heart for being blown off the deck when the Tautog blew a torpedo plane to dogshit right off the bow of the Dolphin. You'll probably get a Bronze Star."

"Any of the other guys would have done the same." He paused and thought about that for a second. "Riggs did."

"He'll get medals too. Or his folks will."

Both men sat in silence thinking about the Riggs family getting that telegram.

23

Patrick tried to change the subject before he started crying. "So the boat wasn't damaged?" asked Patrick.

Halpert grinned and pulled a Lucky Strike from his pack and lit it with his zippo. He snapped it shut and smiled as he inhaled. He exhaled in a cloud of smoke like a dragon and said, "superficial. Nothing that won't keep us from puttin' those sons of bitches at the bottom of the Pacific."

"Good. When can I go back to the boat?" asked Patrick.

"Easy Gunner..." chuckled Halpert. "The Japs aren't going anywhere, and the boat won't be ready for a while yet." He inhaled and blew the smoke out again. "Heal up, and we'll kick some Jap ass soon enough."

Patrick moved his arm in excruciating pain, and he reached out and squeezed Halpert's hand. "I'd salute you, but I don't think I could raise my arm high enough to do a proper salute."

"Don't worry about that, Gunner. Just get back when you are healed. It'll be worse before it gets better."

Halpert squeezed his hand back and stood up. "I have to go write an after-action report. I'll see you tomorrow if I can get away."

"Thanks Chief. I'd like that," Patrick said with a painful grin.

Two days had passed, and Patrick was being released. He had sustained a concussion and superficial burns. He was in pain, but he longed to get back on the boat. Other than the bed he shared with his brother, his cot on the sub was the only bed that he had ever known. It was his bed.

Becky escorted him back to the submarine, and he felt good being in her company. "Am I going to have a bad scar on my eyebrow?" He asked.

She looked at him and tilted her head to the side. "Tell people you got it boxing. It looks like a boxing scar."

"You... know boxing?" he chuckled.

"I do..." she replied in the same mocking tone.

"How do you know boxing?'

"My uncle was a famous boxer." She said with a grin.

"He was? Would I have heard of him?"

"Maybe," she said and looked away.

"Who was he?"

"He was strong. Even when he was old, he was still the strongest man I ever saw. He could pick me up and fly me around, just as light as a feather." She smiled and looked wistfully into the sky.

"Who was he?"

Becky walked silently grinning to add to the torment.

"Who was he? Stop torturing me. I'm a wounded man."

Becky laughed. "Well, my mother's name was Sullivan. So..."

"John L. Sullivan was your uncle?!" he said with eyes as big as saucers.

"He was."

"Will you marry me? You might be the most interesting woman in the world."

Becky burst out laughing. "If I had a dollar for every proposal, I'd be the richest woman in Hawaii."

Patrick laughed. "I suppose you would."

She stopped him and looked into his eyes. "You can write me though. You never know. Just be sure to stay alive."

Patrick smiled. "I'll do that." He thought about kissing her but decided it would be too forward.

"Isn't this your boat?" she asked.

As he approached the Narwhal, he could see most of the crew were busy with repairs and replacing the decking that had been shredded to splinters during the attack.

When he walked across the gangplank, he looked up. They had all stopped what they were doing, and the air became silent except for the sound of water splashing against the hull. Every man was standing at attention with their right hands pressed to their right temple in a sincere salute.

At first Patrick didn't understand what they were doing. Why were they saluting him? He wasn't an officer.

He looked up to see Captain Hendricks on the conning tower with his second in command. Both were at complete attention in a perfect salute. For a moment he panicked, but then instinctively he stopped and returned the salute. The officers snapped their hands to their sides, and the crew did the same. The sound of their arms cutting the wind made a unison whoosh that made Patrick stop and fight to breathe through his emotions. He dropped his salute like he was I a dream.

"As you were!" cried the captain, and the crew resumed their previous work.

"I'll leave you here," said Becky, and Patrick grinned and nodded. She leaned in and kissed his cheek. He winced a little at the pain on his burned skin, but he smiled and watched her walk away. He expected cat calls and other harassment from the crew, but none came. As he looked around, their faces were smiling, and many men nodded with approval. At that moment, he felt that they were his brothers.

When he got to his bunk, there was a bottle of Jameson's lying there with a note.

Enjoy Gunner.
The crew.

He choked up a little and laid down on his bunk, then fell asleep.

When he awoke, the men were clearing the evening mess.

"We saved you some beef and gravy, McGinn," said Torpe-doman Russell.

Patrick sat down and started eating. Beef and beef gravy over rice with bread. He was pretty sure it was old milking cows and not steers, but he didn't care. It was thick and salty and might have been the greatest thing that he had ever eaten.

27

"The old man says that for tonight only, he'll relax the no drinking aboard rule," said the cook.

Patrick looked at the expectant faces and grinned. "Someone go grab it from my footlocker."

In a flash, two men went aft and returned in less than a minute with his bottle of Jameson's and some tin cups.

The men held out their cups, and he poured until the bottle was nearly drained, and he figured there were about two shots left. *Those are for me*, he thought.

"Toast! Toast!" yelled the men.

Patrick thought for a moment, then stood and cleared his throat.

"May your glass always be full. May the roof over your head always be strong."

A sailor named Russell pounded the roof of the sub with two hard blows. "I hope the Christ it's strong," and the men laughed.

Patrick smiled and continued, "And may you be in heaven a half hour before the devil knows you're dead. Slainte M'hath! ...Good health!"

The men raised their cups, and every man drank it down and slammed the tin cups on the steel table with a loud clang that almost sounded harmonious.

As Patrick looked at their faces, he knew. Live or die. He'd be surrounded by brothers.

Four

Mary and the rest of the women were preparing the Sunday dinner. The kitchen and dining room were packed with people and food. The tables were mounded with potatoes and carrots and turnips for boiling and squash and pumpkin for pies. It was going to be a feast, and the scent of clove and nutmeg were heavy in the air.

It was the going away meal for the men and Mary kept the talk focused on cooking and nothing to do with war. They were cooking the biggest turkey they had on the farm and Alston was roasting the front quarter of a doe that he had shot at the end of November.

The family had received a telegram from Patrick saying that he was okay, and his boat would be shipping out as soon as they completed repairs. It was a relief beyond description, but it was short-lived when Mary realized that future telegrams might be accompanied by Father Flynn to give her news that she had lost another child. The very thought of it made her heart ache.

The men were all shipping out to boot camp in the morning, and Mary wanted to enjoy the meal with her children as one family, since it might be the last time that they would all be together. They peeled vegetables and made small talk, but the tension was so thick it was hard to concentrate. Allison was mindlessly kneading biscuit dough when the stress was broken by the sound of a knife being slammed down on the table.

Mary stood frowning. "You're over-working that dough. They'll be hard and flat if you don't stop."

Allison blushed and released the dough ball. "I'm sorry Ma. My mind is elsewhere."

"As we all are." Mary wiped her hands on her apron. "Let's talk about this once and then we'll get it out of our heads for a couple of hours so that we can enjoy this supper." She looked around the room. "Who wants to start?"

Mary glanced from woman to woman. Daisy spoke first. "Mary, you know more than we do. What will we do if God forbid one of them doesn't come home? How do we...?" She broke off and fought back tears.

"Together. That's all I can tell you. If it wasn't for Alder, Finn and Lewin, I don't know how I would have done it. Twelve children and Lillian still on the breast. It was overwhelming at first, but once I knew we wouldn't starve, I could relax and when we made it through that first year, I knew that we would be okay."

Emma cleared her throat. "Da always said to take care of each other because when there is no one else, you need to be able to reach out and help one and other."

Allison snickered. "Easy for you to say. You can reach out to the Morelands, and your husband isn't going."

"That is so unkind. Bill wants to go, but they won't let him because he's deaf in that ear."

Mary gave Allison a long, cold stare. "If you can't be civil, you can walk right back up the road. We'll bring your children back later." Mary had a stare when she was unhappy that felt like she was burning your soul. "Melvin isn't going. Does that make him less of a man?"

Allison stared at the floor and water started to well in her eyes. "I'm sorry Emma. You are right. That was unkind." She sniffled. "I don't even know where my *husband* is. The boys said that they saw him in Watertown, but he went the other way when he saw them. They said he was probably there to enlist." She wiped her eyes on her sleeve and raised her head defiantly. "And I don't care if he ever comes back. He no damn good to us."

Ruth gasped. "Allison, you don't mean that. You're just angry, that's all."

"I am angry. I'm angry he chooses a bottle over his family and I'm angry that those two boys don't have a father to teach them to be a man."

Mary walked to Allison and held her hand. "The boys have plenty of strong men to look up to right out in that barn. Your brothers- and brothers-in-law are all fine men. If Calvin isn't poisoning their lives, then maybe they'll be better off for it."

Allison squeezed her hand and pulled Mary into hug her.

Mary smiled at all the McGinn women, fighting back crying herself. "We'll get through this together. No matter what happens. You are all sisters."

Without a word, she could see the glow of pride on all of them. They were sisters, and they were going to be okay.

Mae leaned in and whispered to Daisy, "See. She's my hero."

"Mind your fire Alston. It's too hot," said Finn. "You'll dry that damned thing out and we'll be having venison jerky."

"Don't tell me how to roast my own meat," replied Alston. "That's why I wrapped it in bacon. The fat protects it from drying out."

Uncle Daniel chuckled. "There, by Jesus, he put you in your place. Good for you Al, stand your ground lad."

Finn knew better than to carry on any further now that Daniel had taken Alston's side. Uncle Daniel was nearing fifty, but he was still the alpha male in the family. He was like a bear in a circus that was pleasant until he was provoked and then he was a savage bear. The boys still talked about the New Year's Eve that Daniel tossed Calving to the wall like a rag doll. The whole event happened so fast that none of them could believe their eyes. Calvin had smashed a bottle and Daniel flew him across the barn like he was lifting a feather pillow and set him straight about drinking.

No one knew where Calvin was now. Alder had felt a little guilty, because it was easier to turn your back on a drunk than to try to get him some help. He had been warned and threatened, but never helped. There was a meeting in Monroe called Alcoholics Anonymous that helped people like Calvin, but no one had offered that up. It was easier to shun him for not handling his liquor than to help him see his problem. Maybe it was because they all drank, but Alder wondered if one day one of them might have the same issue.

They were drinking now. Daniel had two bottles of Irish whiskey that they poured into tin cups and sipped quietly by the fire Alston had made to roast the doe.

They made small talk about the harvest and having enough wood for the winter. It was a bumper crop, and more than enough food was stored for the winter. It was a real concern because in the past, if they were running low on wood, the boys would cut more and if food was running out, one of the older boys would buy some more. What they would not run out of was eggs. Lillian had become obsessed with chickens after winning a blue ribbon at the fair and kept every chick. They produced nearly four dozen eggs a week, and she didn't want anyone to butcher a hen in case she found a champion rooster.

During a small stretch of silence, Bill Moreland cleared his throat. "I'm ashamed I'm not going with you tomorrow. It feels cowardly. But the docs won't clear me."

Alder walked to Bill and put his hand on his shoulder. "No need to apologize, Bill. I'm happy for it. I'm glad someone will help tend to our families if they need anything."

Bill blushed and still felt embarrassed. "I'm going to have Wishe come here to the farm a few times a week to help with firewood and such."

Finn looked at Wishe. He was only a farm hand, but Finn was as close to him as Alder or Lewin. "There's no one I'd trust more with the people I love," said Finn and bowed his head in a nod of respect.

Wishe had his usual expression of a marble statue and returned the bow. His deep brown eyes locked with Finn and never betraying a drop of emotion. "Can I speak?" he asked.

"Of course," said Alder. "You are amongst friends. Speak your mind."

Wishe stepped closer to the fire and looked at the men heading to war. "I was a scout in the Army and I have killed men. Many men. So, hear me now." The only sound was the crackling of the fire and the rhythmic hiss of fat dropping onto the coals. The smoke rose across Wishe's face as if he were an oracle. "When you see the enemy. Do not hesitate. It is unnatural to kill a man, but in war, it must be done. He has a mother and brothers and sisters, and some will have children. But you cannot doubt. Not for a moment. Because in that moment of hesitation, he may deprive you of your mother or brothers or sisters. He may orphan your children."

The faces around the fire were stone like his. "You cannot hesitate. Just kill and ask God for forgiveness later."

The fire crackled and hissed some more, but no one spoke. They just stood with their heads bowed and thought about taking another man's life.

Daniel broke the silence. "Remember the three thousand men at Pearl Harbor. Your brother was one of the injured. Thank Christ, he wasn't one of the dead."

In the days following the attack, Germany declared war on the U.S. and now they knew that they were all-in. There was no going back now until the job was done.

Daniel studied each man. They all had a look of resolve. Except for Lewin. "Lew. What's wrong?" he asked.

"I'm scared." Lewin admitted sheepishly.

"Don't worry about that, son. They'll fix that in boot camp." This got a chuckle from everyone. "Be sure to make love to your wives tonight. It will be the last time for a long time for the lot of you. Of course, Alston, you'll still have your hand." This brought a roar from the group and the tension was released like air from a balloon.

"Very funny Uncle. I'm giving you the burnt end of this girl," he said as he turned the spit again.

The mood lightened, and the talk returned to their normal banter until the sound of Mary calling them to eat brought the talk to an end.

It was a great feast, and every man kept close to his wife, knowing it might be their last meal together.

The next morning, Bill and Wishe drove the men to Watertown, where they boarded a train with a hundred other men heading off to war. The women had all said their goodbyes and agreed that it might be easier to see them off from home rather than at a train station. That would be saved for their homecomings.

Five

E mma sat in her window at the Moreland General Store, sewing a child's dress of red velvet for the holidays. It had a white lace collar and a neat white fringe on the cuffs and hem, but she wasn't sure who would buy it. With most of the working men gone from the area, shopping had slowed dramatically. She was just happy to be busy. It kept her mind from dwelling on the men that had gone away.

From time to time, her mind drifted to the sickening feeling of killing Albert Merrill. She kept telling herself that she had to do it to survive, but then she thought about her brothers and wondered if they would have to kill as well. *Maybe men don't care about that*, she thought. But unlike most women, she had killed and had felt the anguish that came with it. *Stick to your sewing,* she thought and continued to make the dress.

About a week after everyone left, she was working and didn't notice anyone walking to the store until she heard the familiar ring of the front doorbell. She looked up and saw Earl Merrill standing before her with his hat in his right hand and his left arm dangling without life.

He glanced down sheepishly at her and cleared his throat. "Excuse me ma'am. Is Mr. Moreland here?"

Emma sat in bewilderment at seeing him. He had always been a decent customer, but she had killed his brother. *What in God's name could he want from Bill*, she wondered, but put down her sewing and called out to the back room where Bill was conducting an inventory of their stock. "Bill! There's someone here to see you!" She couldn't think of anything to say, so they just stared at each other, wondering what the other was thinking.

Bill came to the front and laid his clipboard on the counter. "Earl, what can I do for you?" Bill had always liked Earl, but ever since the incident with Albert, he became leery of everyone's intentions.

Earl squeezed the hat in his hand and still watched the floor. Emma realized that he was simply nervous. "Well, Mr. Moreland, sir. I'd like to enquire about work. Since all the *able* men went away, it only leaves guys like me to work," he said, pointing at his left arm. "I'm not much for lifting anymore, but I could fill a car with gas with one arm."

Emma noticed for the first time since he had come into the store that he was thin. Very thin. Like a skeleton. Suddenly, her apprehension was gone, and she wanted to help him.

Bill seemed to be thinking it over. It was probably only a few seconds, but to Emma, it felt like an eternity. "Oh Bill. Please give him some work. He's not his brother. He's a kind man. Finn said so himself."

Bill studied Emma and realized that she was the type of gal who was a saver. She liked animals and birds and people in general. She had a big heart and wanted to help anyone in need. Even the brother of Albert Merrill. "Earl, you came at a good time. We do need help across the street."

Earl lifted his gaze from the floor and smiled. "Thank you. I promise. I won't let you down, sir."

Bill reached out to shake his hand. "Earl, you're a fair bit older than me, so please stop calling me sir. Bill will do fine. If my father shows up, that's the real Mr. Moreland. You can call him sir if you want."

Earl smiled. "Thanks Bill. When would you like me to start work?"

Bill checked the clock. It was 9:45. "How about in fifteen minutes? Or are you busy today? You can start in the morning if you want."

Earl's smile grew from ear to ear. "No sir. I mean no Bill. I can start now."

"Excellent. Have you had breakfast yet?"

"No, I haven't. I'm down to potatoes at night, then maybe refried potatoes the next day. But last night I ate all of my potatoes."

Bill patted him on the shoulder and smiled. "Well, I'll come with you, and they'll set you up with sandwiches on the days you work. If you come in early, they'll feed you eggs, toast and coffee. Those are part of the deal. We'll feed you and we don't take it out of your pay. So long as people don't take advantage."

"Wow. Thank you so much. I appreciate it, Bill." Earl seemed so excited that he might jump out of his skin.

"Us un-ables, need to stick together."

Earl looked at Bill and then to Emma. "I'm sorry Albert did what he did to you. He was a bad man. I tried to stop him."

Bill pointed to his dead arm. "We know. And I'm sorry he did that to you. Finn always said that you weren't like him, and you were a worker."

"Albert was a decent worker when we were kids, but somewhere along the way, he took a turn and found it easier to steal than look for work, I guess. But we were raised right." Earl smiled silently to himself, recollecting his parents. "My folks would turn in their graves knowing how he turned out. My mother never missed a Sunday service at church unless we were snowed in and then she read the bible all afternoon. She was a god-fearin' woman. Albert never feared God."

"He's likely burning in hell," Emma hissed.

Earl nodded. "Probably. He wasn't always bad, but he was bad at the end. So let him take his medicine down there."

They were about to leave when Emma noticed the state of Earl's clothing. They were dirty and were patched with an old handkerchief that was sewn together very roughly. "Do you have much in the way of clothes, Earl?"

"I have another pair of trousers and a couple of shirts. Why do you ask?"

"Well, bring me your extra clothes and I'll mend them for you."

"Thank you, Mrs. Moreland. I'd appreciate that. My tailoring skills are what they used to be," he said, pointing at the dead arm.

Emma was embarrassed that she had mentioned it. She felt like none of her brothers would be able to sew one handed. "Please call me Emma. I'll set you up well. Anything that needs mending."

"Come on," said Bill. "Let's get you fed." Bill opened the door for Earl and the two men headed across the road to the diner.

Later that afternoon, Wishe arrived with butchered hogs from the Moreland farm with two other men. "Unload into the cooler and I'll be in to help in a minute."

The two hands didn't balk at the order and went to work unloading the truck.

"Miss Emma. How are you?" he asked.

Emma smiled and remembered the day that a farmhand had made a crude remark to her and Wishe struck him in the mouth and took away his biscuits. Before then, she was afraid of him because he always seemed so serious. Since then, she had always had an affection for him and his presence always made her feel safe. "I'm well and you?"

"Good. It's more work with so many gone. But I'm happy to be here."

"Do you feel like you wanted to go with them?" she asked.

"No. I served, and that was enough. I am too old to be drafted now. War is a young man's world."

She put down her sewing and stared into his eyes. "Are they going to be alright? My brothers and Joe. Will they be alright?"

Wishe stood silently for a moment, considering an answer that might make her feel better, but then decided that the truth was always best. "I cannot say. When so many men go to war, many will die. Sometimes it's luck that lets you survive. Sometimes skill." He could sense her anxiety, but it was best to prepare her for whatever might come. "I had two brothers. They died in France. They were both younger. None of us had taken wives yet. I miss them. But they will know no more pain. So that makes my heart happy."

Emma's anxiety turned to sadness. "I never knew. I'm sorry."

"They were good men." Wishe thought for a moment. "Your brothers are fighters, and Joe is strong. Very strong. That will help them. If you ask me in my heart, then I say yes. They will come back to us."

"Did you think that about your brothers?" she asked.

"No. They were for slaughter. I was a scout, so my job was to be unseen. They were infantry with no place to hide. They would be part of the numbers."

"Numbers? I don't understand."

"In war, soldiers are numbers. You are in the number of killed. The number of wounded or the number that comes home." As he spoke, his eyes started to glisten with tears, but he didn't cry. "Your brothers will be in the number that comes home." He wasn't sure that he believed that, but he felt like she needed to hear it.

Emma felt tears well in her eyes as well and nodded. "Thank you, Wishe."

"I have to help unload," he said and walked to the back of the store.

She sat and stared out the window at nothing and prayed to God to bring them all back safely.

Six

Lewin has been a farmer for his whole life, so the physical part of boot camp was a breeze. The hardest thing for him to get used to was all the yelling. He couldn't recall his father ever raising his voice and when his mother was upset, she usually did her management with a look.

As he low crawled under the barbed wire, his pants became entangled and he found himself caught with his backside in the air, suspended from a barb.

"God dammit McGinn you simple son of a bitch! Get your ass down! It's been shot off!" Sergeant McCrory was a hard man. His face was like wrinkled leather from years in the field, but the most unnerving thing was a scar running through his eyebrow and cheek. It was from a saber cut in the great war and when he glared, it made him seem even more fierce.

He jerked himself free and heard his pants rip in the process.

"That's government property, McGinn. Do you imagine we have tailors waiting to fix your God damn drawers! Move it!"

He moved as fast as he could and as he saw the end of the obstacle; the ground became softer, and it was like he was crawling through pudding.

"Hurry! Hurry! Faster now! Move your asses, ladies!" McCrory bellowed.

As he exited the wire, he jumped to his feet and started to run. His heart was pounding, and the mud was so thick, it was like wearing a bear's skin.

"McGinn Halt!"

He stopped in his tracks and took a position of attention.

"Weapon, check McGinn!" McCrory snatched the rifle from his hands and peered at the end of the barrel. "You're KIA you dumb shit. Killed in action! This rifle is completely plugged! It's going to blow up in your face and if that doesn't kill you, the German bastard bearing down on you sure as shit will!"

Lewin stood there, not knowing what to say. He was sure the Sergeant was right, but he wanted to get away while he still had a little dignity left.

"KP McGinn. If you can't keep your weapon clean, maybe you can learn on dishes. Move out!" He slammed the rifle into Lewin's chest and moved on to the next target. Lewin finished the course and joined the group of men who had already completed.

A private named Leeman whispered to him. "Don't let it bother you, McGinn. He seems hard, but he's just trying to keep us alive."

45

Lewin nodded in a way that said "thanks" without looking. Chit-chat in formation was good for at least fifty push-ups and Lewin's chest still hurt from his seemingly endless trail of screw-ups. His thoughts drifted to home and what he might write in a letter to Cecelia. Certainly, he wouldn't tell her about anything heroic, but he didn't want to inform her about being a screw-up either. He wondered how the others were doing in their boot camps. Alder and Joe were in the Army too, but they were at different camps in New York and New Jersey, and Finn had joined the Marines, so he was somewhere in South Carolina. Lewin imagined it was a hell of a lot warmer than Danvers, Massachusetts. He knew they'd be fine. Alder had always been a leader of sorts, and Finn and Joe were both tough as nails. For Joe's size, he might have been the strongest man Lewin had ever met. Joe was able to walk on his hands for a hundred feet or so. Lewin doubted men in the circus were able to walk that far.

The rest of the day was mundane Army training. Classes before and after chow, then a few minutes to write home, followed by lights out. Lewin slept well. He couldn't even remember waking to roll over. In his dreams, he was pulled close to Cecelia, trying to generate heat between their bodies to stay warm in the upstairs bedroom. He kept thinking the fire must have gone out and was why he was so cold. *I'll need to be up early and start the fire*, he thought, *so Cecelia and the children won't be cold*. He snuggled closer to her and felt the warmth of her body next to him, and he smiled. He loved her completely, and she loved him.

"McGinn," a man's voiced hissed into his ear. "Wake up. KP."

Cecelia faded away and he felt the chill of the barracks on his face and realized he was a long way from home. He jumped up and went quietly to the latrine to clean up, then headed to his footlocker to dress. He had gotten used to dressing in the dark. One of the benefits about the Army was that everybody dressed the same.

When he arrived at the Mess Hall, a fat burley cook named Puzzi greeted him. "Well, you must be McGinn. Have you ever cooked before, McGinn?" Puzzi wore a greasy cook's jacket and had a fat cigar in his mouth.

"Yes, sir."

He smiled and tapped the ash from the cigar into his hand. "Sir? Jesus, man, learn your ranks. They don't have any officers cooking; I can assure you. Corporal will do, or just call me Puzzi."

"Okay Puzzi, what would you like me to do?"

"Start peeling potatoes. You Irish are always good for that," he said with a chuckle.

"Yes, Corporal." Lewin started toward the kitchen and then stopped. "Where are the potatoes?"

"Next to the onions," he said with a wicked grin and jerked a thumb to a table with bags of potatoes and onions piled four sacks high.

Lewin's heart sunk. *There must be two-hundred pounds of each, easier to peel them than to dig them up*, he thought. As he

47

peeled his potatoes, he kept smelling an acrid smell that was something akin to a fart, but it smelled more chemical than that. When the Corporal stopped to view his progress, Lewin asked about the smell.

Puzzi laughed it off and said that it was probably him. They had served beans last night and since he had broken his nose fighting several times, he really couldn't smell anything. "Besides, Puzzi means stinky in Italian!" he roared with laughter.

Lewin smiled at that, but after Puzzi was gone, he could still smell the odor. He had thought that maybe it was from boiled eggs, but they mostly ate scrambled and that was the case today. Two men stood cracking egg after egg into a large mixing bowl.

"Come on gents. Fire those stove tops. The troops will be expecting hot chow."

As one of the men cracking eggs walked to the stove, he stopped and sniffed the air. "Hey Puzzi, something is not right. It smells like gas over here," he said.

"Really?" Puzzi said and walked toward the stove with his cigar still on his lips, when the stove exploded in a hail of metal and glass.

Lewin saw Puzzi, and the other man torn to shreds before his eyes. The thought to run to help them but fell flat on his face. His leg screamed with pain, and he tried to rise. His right pant leg was red from the knee down and blood was pumping from a wound. He was scared and didn't know what to do until the other soldier breaking eggs pushed him to the ground and started ripping the belt from his waist. "Lay down McGinn! You're bleeding to death!"

Lewin gazed at the ceiling in confusion and tried to think of home. He felt the belt tightening around his thigh, and soon there was a clamor of activity all about him. The soldier grabbed his collar and started dragging him toward the door. He started drifting off to sleep when he was shocked to consciousness by the barking of Sergeant McCrory. "Jesus H. Christ! Get a medic up here for McGinn this instant."

Lewin opened his eyes to see McCrory looking down at him. "McGinn. Talk to me, son. You need to stay awake. We're going to get you help in a minute. But you have to keep your eyes open."

"Yes. Sergeant," Lewin mumbled and closed his eyes.

He was awakened again by McCrory physically shaking him. "Come on McGinn. You with me? What's your wife's name, McGinn?"

This puzzled him a bit, and he roused his mind to a state of mild alertness. "Cecelia, Sergeant."

"Is she a good woman?"

Lewin thought for a moment and a little grin crossed his face and he did feel a little more alert. "The very best."

"You're a luck man McGinn, you'll likely be seeing her before you know it." McCrory patted him on the shoulder and two orderlies from the hospital slid him on to a canvas stretcher.

"We'll take him from here, Sergeant," said the one at his head. "We'll take good care of you," he said.

49

The orderly's upside-down face changed to Cecelia's smiling face and wondered how he'd see her as his mind drifted into darkness.

Seven

C ecelia filled the kitchen stove with wood and set a kettle on for tea. The January winds whipped the side of the house, and all the windows were painted in intricate frost patterns like beautiful white leaves. The winter had been particularly cold, and she wasn't sure how she would get more wood if she ran out, so she moved the bedrooms downstairs to help conserve on wood. She and her mother Laurel had moved the children's beds to the living room, and she slept on the daybed that served as a couch.

As a child, she could remember napping on the day bed between milkings and how her adopted father Wilbur had called her lazy for sleeping during the day. But he was gone now, and she felt a warmth in her heart that he was probably burning in hell.

While the children still slept, she went to the shed to carry in a basket of wood. It was times like these that she missed Lewin the most. She hadn't fetched wood more than a couple

51

of times since they moved into their home and between him and Edmund. Neither had her mother, Laurel. The men always made sure thier families were taken care of.

Before Edmund went off to war with the rest of the men, he had met a lovely woman with a beautiful smile named Doreen Howes. She might have been the happiest woman that Cecelia had ever met. She was the oldest daughter of a local farmer, and she and Edmund had hit it off at once. Doreen came almost every day to help tend to the children and Cecelia considered her a sister as much as the McGinn women who had been so welcoming to her.

Doreen always smiled... always. She was fascinated by Edmund's passion for bees, and they tended his hives together to make bee's wax candles and honey for extra money. Edmund had become an expert beekeeper and had more than fifty hives spread around the local farms. Most farmers were happy to have the hives since their crops did so much better with an active hive nearby. But this was winter, and the bees were safe in hibernation until the spring. That left Doreen with extra time on her hands, so she preferred to spend it visiting and knitting with Cecelia.

Cecelia could hear a car coming down the road and rubbed the frost off from the window, expecting Doreen to be coming for tea and toast. As the frost turned to water, she instead, saw a dark sedan with a star on the side. *An Army car*, she thought. Her heart began pounding, and she found it hard to take in enough air to breathe. She watched it rumbling down the frozen dirt road. She wondered, was the car was slowing or was it heading to her mother's house. No one had been to war yet that she knew of, but the news reports always seemed to be delayed by a couple of weeks. Her eyes burned and filled with tears as the car slowed and turned into the driveway, it made her feel as if she might melt into a puddle on her kitchen floor.

She peeked in at the children, who were still asleep, and tried to stiffen herself as she heard the car door shut and the sound of boots on her front porch. She couldn't breathe at all and wiped her hands on her shirt. A single silhouette appeared in the front door window. When the knock came, it seemed quite loud, and she rushed to the door before the visitor knocked again. When she opened the door, a tall, thin man in civilian clothes was standing before her with an envelope in his hand.

"Mrs. McGinn?" the man asked, hopeful, not sure he had the correct address.

"Yes," Cecelia croaked and bit her lip to fight back tears.

"I have a telegram for Cecelia McGinn from Lewin McGinn."

Cecelia finally was able to breathe. She reached out and took the envelope. "Thank you," she whispered. The man smiled and nodded a goodbye, then headed for his car.

She closed the door and tore the envelope open.

DEAREST CECELIA... I HAVE BEEN INJURED IN AN EXPLOSION... MY RIGHT LEG WAS BADLY INJURE D... BUT THE DOCS SAY I WILL LIVE AND I WILL BE

COMING HOME WHEN THEY ARE SURE THE LEG IS
SAFE... I WILL WRITE SOON. LOVE LEWIN

A flood of relief came over her entire body. "Thank you,
Lord," she said aloud, looking at the ceiling. Tears started pouring from her eyes. Tears of relief. She wondered about the state
of his leg, but just having him home would be reward enough.
Regardless of his physical state. Ellie started to stir, and she
plucked her up and pulled her tight, kissing her over and over.

When Lewin woke up at the base hospital, his leg was killing
him. It felt heavy and ached to the bone. He reached down to
scratch his thigh that was itching like crazy, only to discover the
heavy plaster of a full leg cast. He tried to move the blanket and
sheet, but he was still a little drowsy and flopped at it in vain.

"Hey, don't do that," he heard a voice call out.

A moment later, an Orderly was at his bedside. He was a
broad chested black man with arms so big he looked like a strong
man in the circus. Lewin stared in wonderment for a minute
and realized that he had never talked to a black man in person.
In fact, he had never even seen a black person before except in
movies.

"I want to look at my leg," Lewin croaked in a hoarse whisper.

"I'm afraid there's not much to see except a big cast," he said. He saw the man's name stenciled on his fatigues. It read *Armstrong*, and that made Lewin smile.

"I like your name."

Armstrong wrinkled his brow and looked at Lewin expecting it was some jape. "My name?"

"Yeah, Arm-strong. You have the biggest damned arms I have ever seen."

Armstrong relaxed and smiled. "Railroad work does that to a man. Driving spikes and straightening ties all day."

"Where are you from?" asked Lewin.

"I'm from a town called Monroe, North Carolina. It's near Charlotte. You?"

Lewin laughed aloud, "Monroe, Maine."

"Well, I'll be, small world," he said with a smile. "Do you still want a look at that cast?"

"Yes please."

Armstrong carefully moved the blanket and sheet to avoid jostling the cast. Lewin looked in amazement at the long white cast that covered his entire leg except for his toes. Armstrong reached down and gently touched his toes. "Can you feel me touching your toes?"

"Yes. Why?"

"I'm just making sure you have feeling and blood flow to your toes. If they put the cast on too tight, your leg could swell and the flesh will dies pretty fast, so they'd amputate."

Lewin's eyes widened. "How do you know that?"

55

"The Army taught me. That and all kinds of other stuff."

"Does it look okay? I can't really see it from here."

"Looks like a broken leg. Your leg was stove up bad when they brought you in. It was headed in two different directions with a huge gash through your thigh. Lucky you didn't bleed to death."

Lewin thought for a moment and remembered the other soldier on KP who had wrapped the belt around his leg to control the bleeding. "Yeah. I guy saved my leg and Sarge McCrory was there. He wasn't yelling at me, so I remember thinking it must be bad."

"Were you much of a dancer, McGinn?"

"Dancer?"

"Yeah, you know, did you like to dance with your wife?"

Lewin grimaced a little. "To tell the truth, I'm not really much of a dancer at all"

"Well, I supposed there's no great loss on that front. They said this might take months, if not years, to fully heal."

"Years?"

"Yeah. We'll get you on your feet again, and then you'll be going home. But I dare say you'll never dance for shit again."

It took a moment for that to sink in. He'd be going home, and he hadn't even finished boot camp. He felt a little ashamed and lucky all at the same time.

Armstrong started rearranging the sheet and blanket, when they heard a bellowing from a few beds down. "Boy! I need a bedpan!" Armstrong bit his lip and shook his head, "a foot of cock, ten pounds of balls and enough hair on my chest to knit a Navajo rug and he calls me boy? Shit, he must call an alligator a lizard."

That made Lewin laugh. "What's your first name?"

"Amos. You?"

"Lewin."

"Come on, boy! I'm going to shit the bed!"

"I'll catch you later Lewin. Duty calls. It makes them feel important to boss us about." He smiled and winked at Lewin. In a flash, he turned and ran toward the bellowing man. "Oh, I's so sorry, boss. Here's I come boss. I got you a bedpan." Doing his best Amos Jones impersonation from the Amos and Andy radio show.

Later that afternoon, Amos returned. "Lewin. How are you doing?"

"I'm okay. Bored mostly."

"I'm about to head to chow. My shift is almost over. Anything I can do for you? Something you need?"

Lewin thought about it for a moment. "Maybe some paper to send letters and a magazine."

Amos smiled. "I can do that. But don't expect anything too racy on the magazine front. They don't want black men even looking at pictures of white women and getting any wrong ideas."

Lewin realized how sheltered his life in Maine was from the real world. "You know that you are the first black person I have ever talked to?"

"You, for real? There ain't no black people in Maine?"

"I'm not sure. I imagine there might be in the southern part of the state. Just not where I live. We have Indians, but no blacks."

Amos thought about that. "Must be too damned cold. We're a hot weather people you know."

They both laughed at that. Amos grew serious. "My pappy taught me to treat a man like a man. Like a gentleman. If he returns it, then you'll tend to get along. If he doesn't, then don't pay him no mind. He ain't worth your time. Black or white."

Lewin smiled. "My Da used to say something along those lines as well."

Amos nodded. "There you go, black, white, makes no difference. The best fathers try to teach their sons what's right."

"Well, go to chow while it's still hot. And thank you."

"I'll see you tomorrow, McGinn. I'll find you some letter writing gear."

The men shook hands and Amos left. That night as Lewin laid in bed trying to sleep, he thought about his brothers and about Amos. He tried to imagine if someone had called Finn, *boy*. Would they still have any teeth left? After a while he realized that he just missed his family and drifted off to sleep.

Eight

M ae finished her shift at the hospital and made her way to the apartment that she and Finn had rented before he left for the war. It was a modest place with a three-season porch on both floors. She loved the porch. Every night when the weather permitted, she and Finn would spend their evenings there listening to the radio and having drinks. But mostly they talked.

They talked about everything. They talked about Jim and Alvin. They talked about growing up with so many siblings, or in her case, no siblings. They talked about their future and how many children would be enough and what they might name them. If they were to have a boy, then Michael after her father and grandfather. If it was a girl, they had discussed Marion. It was a way to name her after Mary, without actually calling her Mary. But Mae won out and the first girl would simply be called Mary after her hero.

As she walked up the steps, she could see an envelope poking out of the top of the slot. *God, not another bill*, she hoped. But as she came closer, she could see Finn's writing on the return address and her heart leaped for joy. She flipped the mailbox open so hard that she might have ripped the cover off from its hinges.

The lighting was poor and made it hard to read, so she ran upstairs and immediately sat at her kitchen table. She could feel something in the envelope, so she carefully opened the flap to prevent injuring the contents.

There was a letter of several pages in length and a few photographs. The first one was of Finn in his dress uniform. Mae loved the uniform and Finn was so handsome in the photo. His smile made her feel happy, but then it made her miss him even more.

The next photo was of him, and four other men dressed in battle fatigues and rifles with bayonets fixed and the men all seemed to about to attack the camera. The writing on the back said *Hell's Fury Squad: Smith, O'Shea, Lynch, McIntyre and me. Parris Island, 1942.*

The 3rd photo was a great surprise. It was a picture of Finn with Johnny Roy at the beach in California. She was happy to see John and would be sure to share it with Ruth and Joe's family, but them being in California meant that their time to leave was growing near. He hadn't even told her that he was going there until he arrived at Camp Pendleton. John was in the 1st Battalion of the 5th Marine Regiment and Finn had been assigned to the 3rd Battalion of the same Regiment so they were trying to stay in contact with each other as much as they could. It was a link to home for each of them.

The final picture was of Finn laying in the sand with just a tank top on. He was smiling at the camera and pointing at writing in the sand. It was a heart with the words; *I LOVE YOU MAE* drawn inside of the heart. She studied the photo and felt her heart ache at how much she missed him, and she kissed it.

The letter was full of small talk, and he related the story of taking a train all the way across country with Marines crammed ass to elbow for most of the trip. He said that his favorite moments were when he would step onto the platform between cars and have a smoke. It always reminded him of the porch, and he would imagine that she was there with him, telling him about her day or planning details about a baby's nursery. That made her appreciate the porch even more, and she heated some ginger ale on the stove and poured a drop of whiskey into it. She sat on the porch sipping her drink and reading, then re-reading the letter over and over until the drink was gone.

The troopship carrying them across the Pacific wreaked of cigarette smoke and body odor. The cargo holds that had once held supplies were now row after row of berths from floor to ceiling stacked five high. Finn was on a bottom berth, which was nice that he didn't have to climb just to get in and out of bed, but it was a place where everybody congregated, so there was never any privacy. He was thankful that he was not a top bunk guy, because everything in the air tended to rise making the air hard to take between heat, smoke, and bodily functions. Sometimes the air was so putrid it made it hard for Finn to breathe. He would get onto the deck any chance he could and spent his time in the fresh air as much as they would let him, but every night it was back to the stink-hole.

John Roy was on a different ship, so he didn't have anyone close around him. There were plenty of guys to talk with, but he liked John, and it reminded him of home to be around him. One night when he was coming back from the head, a couple of guys were gathered at his bunk laughing. He started to hear the conversation, and realized they were reading his letter from Mae. He had slipped it under his pillow to read again before bed and he could feel his blood boil.

"Something interesting boys?" he said through gritted teeth.

A Chicago guy named Hansen held the picture of Mae and was using it to fan his face. He had pockmarked skin and a ruddy complexion. In some ways, he was the picture of how Finn imagined the Nazis to look with his blond hair and blue eyes. "Oh, McGinn. You lucky bastard. I'd like to borrow this, but I doubt you'd part with it."

"Give me the picture, Hansen." Finn said and held out his hand.

"Uhhh, I don't know McGinn. I'd only need it for a couple of minutes. She wouldn't take me long at all."

The thought of this jackass pleasuring himself to Mae's picture was pushing him to a boiling point. But then he realized that Hansen was just seeing how far he could push Finn and felt safe because of these two buddies hanging there with him.

"Wives are off limits, Hansen. You know that. Girlfriends and mothers are fair game. But nobody wants mothers, especially yours, since most of the guys on this boat probably already had her. Now give me the picture."

"Or what McGinn? What the hell are you going to do about it?" Hansen puffed his chest up and drove the point of his chin out, almost daring Finn to strike him.

"They eat a lot of rice where we're going. That'll be lucky for you. Because if I don't have that picture in my hand in one second, I'm going to knock some of your teeth out."

Hansen opened his mouth and the word "try", escaped one second before Finn snapped off a jab that struck Hansen full in the mouth."

Hansen stood in stunned disbelief, and Finn snatched the picture from his hand. Hansen leaned forward, spat a glob of blood onto the deck. "What the fuck. I was just kidding, McGinn!"

"I wasn't," Finn replied and watched cautiously for a response from Hansen or his cronies. "Wives are off limits, so find some other ways to get your jollies."

Hansen spat again. "You sucker punched me. You sneaky bastard."

"Well, if you want to go again. Just say so and we'll have a scrap. But I'm telling you. I won't be gentle like last time."

"No one is going again," called a voice from behind Finn. In all the chaos with Hansen, Finn didn't realize that they had drawn a crowd of fight-goers. The voice belonged to a big Sergeant from Wisconsin named Baer, but the guys all called him Griz. Short for grizzly.

Hansen appealed to Baer and started pleading his case. "Griz. We were just friggin' around with McGinn. We didn't mean anything by it."

Baer took a deep breath and exhaled. "I'm married and if you would have pulled that stunt with me, I would have unscrewed your pin head and stuffed it up your ass. Wives are off limits. Got it?" Baer glared around at all the men present. "That goes for all of you. When you're married someday, you'll understand. Now fuck off back to your racks."

Everyone dispersed and Baer turned to Finn. "May I?" he said and held a hand out for the picture. Finn slowly handed it over. Baer studied the picture and nodded approval. "She's a fine woman, McGinn. You're a lucky guy," and handed the photo back. "Make sure you go back in one piece to her."

"I will, Sergeant," he replied.

"When it's you and I, Grizz will do." Baer patted him on the shoulder and walked away.

Finn climbed into his rack to read the letter again and the guy in the bunk above him, Alfred Dumond, leaned over and peeked over the edge of the bed at him. "I had your back, McGinn. If anything happened with the other two guys, I would have jumped in."

"Thanks Freddy. I appreciate that."

"Hey us Maine guys have to stick together against these city boys." Dumond was from the southern part of the state, nearer to the New Hampshire border, and once Finn found out, he tried to take him under his wing. Dumond was twenty and seemed to be a capable man. Finn just worried how he might react when the real shit started. It's easier to talk about taking a man's life than to actually pull the trigger.

"You still single Freddy?"

"Yeah, I'm afraid so. I haven't had much time for courting lately," he said with a big smile.

"Do you have any girl to write to?"

"Just my Ma and sisters."

"Write to my sister Frances. She's a sweet girl and a looker to boot."

"Do you have a picture?"

"No. God knows what they'd do with it on this floating shithouse."

Dumond thought for a moment. "Yes, I will write to her. I'll believe you on the looks and it will be a surprise when I see it."

"I'll tell her you'll be writing, and I'll give you the address in the morning."

"Thanks McGinn. You're a pal."

Finn smiled. "Well, it's like you said. Us Maine guys have to stick together."

Dumond smiled and his face disappeared as he rolled back onto his bunk.

Finn read the letter one more time and closed his eyes, trying to picture Mae so that he might dream of her.

Nine

B oot camp had been a walk in the park for Joe. The physical parts were far less strenuous than handling a two-man saw or a cant dog. A cant dog was a long pole with a spike and a hook at the end to be able to move logs around in the woods. In many ways, having a bayonet on his rifle reminded him of it.

He excelled at moving through the woods quickly, and he had become an expert shot. Better than his hunting skills back in Maine. The day he had enlisted he was approached by the man in the Navy suit, it turned out he was part of a new covert operation called the Office of Strategic Services or O.S.S. for short, and Joe was to be a candidate due to his fluent French and physical strength. They were commandos, and they were being trained to wreak havoc behind enemy lines.

When Joe was a kid, his father used black powder to blow up big rocks, but the Army had much better explosives and Joe was enjoying blowing things up. The Army was teaching them how to find the weak points in a structure. He had never really been a fighter. He had been in a few scraps, but only kid stuff. He surprised himself at how much he liked the hand-to-hand training, and he could handle himself well.

The part that excited him most was that he was going to be trained as a paratrooper and jump out of airplanes. He would have done it for the thrill of it, but the Army would pay him fifty dollars more a month and he certainly wasn't going to refuse the money.

They started in classes, learning all the technical aspects of a parachute. Then they practiced landing by jumping from a platform. The first time he tried it, he landed awkwardly and turned his ankle a little. But by the third time, it was becoming fun for him. It was fun until the first live jump, where he was a little anxious. Joe had been promoted to Sergeant, and he was now the squad leader for the jump and his job was to follow the officer out the door, making him the second man on the ground. Their platoon leader was a West Point man from Michigan named Captain Kellogg. The men referred to him as Corn Flakes behind his back because Michigan was where Corn Flakes were made. All in all, he seemed like a pretty steady guy. That was, until his first jump.

The message came from the cockpit that they would be over the drop zone in one minute. The Call "Stand up!" ran up the line. "Hook up!" followed, and the men latched a carabiner onto the cable running overhead.

A second call rang out. "Thirty seconds!" and men started shuffling to toward the door.

"Green light in ten seconds sir!" Joe yelled to Kellogg, who looked like he had seen a ghost. Joe peeked out the door and the ground seemed a hell of a long way down. Then the light changed.

"Green light! Go sir!" shouted Joe. Kellogg stood in the doorway, paralyzed with fear. Joe could feel men crowding him from behind and after a couple more seconds, he shoved Kellogg from the plane, waited a beat and followed him.

The chute deployed seconds after leaving the plane and Joe tensed as he fell. He struggled to breathe and grasped the handles that helped him to steer tightly. He tugged a couple of times. The chute responded, and he exhaled. Then he relaxed and smiled and enjoyed the ride to the ground.

After the men had all landed safely they returned to the base and Kellogg summoned him to his office.

Joe entered his office and stood at attention. "Sergeant Roy reporting as ordered, sir."

"At ease, Roy." Kellogg said as he sifted through reports on his desk. His office was small and had one window. He had a desk fan, but it wasn't helping to ease the stuffiness of the thick southern air.

Joe relaxed and stood with his arms still at his side. Kellogg couldn't have been more than thirty, but he was already showing signs of a receding hairline. Like most West Point graduates Joe had met, he was meticulous in his appearance. He was very fit and appeared like he was poured into his uniform.

Kellogg studied Joe "Did you push me from the plane?"

Joe wasn't sure how to respond, but yes, probably wouldn't be a great answer. "No sir. I stumbled when the men behind me pushed forward."

Kellogg studied Joe for a moment. "You're sure you didn't push me?"

"Yes sir. I think I bumped you just as you were jumping, but I didn't push you." Joe tried not to make eye contact in case Kellogg might see through his deception.

"I only ask because it might undermine morale if the men think I'm afraid to jump. Do you catch my meaning?"

Joe tried to think quickly. "Yes, sir," he responded. "You were the first one out the door. Everyone knows it." Joe didn't actually know what the men had seen. They wore so much gear that most men just focused on the back of the man in front of them, but he was fairly certain no one had seen him push Kellogg.

"Well, we will be jumping again in the morning. Tell them men not to crowd you."

"Yes, sir."

"I'll see you in the morning, Roy. Get some rest and tell the men, great job."

"Thank you, sir. I will, sir."

"Dismissed."

As Joe spun on his heels to leave, Kellogg spoke again. "And Roy."

Joe stopped and faced the captain.

"Thank you."

Joe nodded without speaking and left. The air outside was hotter than his office, but there was enough of a breeze to make it tolerable.

The next morning, they had their second jump and when the light turned green, Kellogg was gone with Joe on his tail. First time jitters, Joe thought.

Ruth walked down West Road toward the diner. She liked working there, and it had become a family enterprise. Emma was across the street at the store and Allison came daily to bring baked good from the Moreland farm. Frances had started working at the Moreland house as soon as she was done school. It was still funny at times to think of the animosity between the McGinns' and the Morelands' from her childhood, but she liked them, and Miss Rose was excellent to work for. Sometimes, when the cleaning was done, she would have Ruth come sit with her and talk about life in general. Mr. Moreland was gone most of the time on business, and Ruth figured she kept a housekeeper to help curb her loneliness.

Today she was working the lunch and dinner shift at the diner. It was strange with so many men off to war, people weren't eating out as much. There were more women stopping in groups, and Ruth liked to hear them gossip. She knew it was wrong, but somehow it thrilled her to know a tidbit about someone else.

As she waited tables, she heard a group of women talking about Virgil Orwell, the man who owned Orwell shoes where her mother worked. One of the women said he had his wife committed to a mental asylum called the Golden Institute in Watertown so he could have an affair with his secretary.

At first, there was a sense of excitement in hearing gossip, but then a sense of guilt for hearing such a thing and tried to avoid the table. But it was a small diner and then she heard that women in town were already having affairs with men who didn't go to war while their husbands were away. One, Ethel Miller, became pregnant a month after her husband left and now, she was going to try to pass the child off as his. He was in the Army like Joe and was in Georgia preparing for war.

She felt sorry for Mr. Miller, whoever he was, and it made her miss Joe even more. He sent letters, but they were always cryptic. He didn't say where he was or what he was doing, only that he was training. He told stories about other men and sometimes she thought she knew more about them than her own husband. She never doubted his fidelity, because Joe was such a devout man, but she wondered why everything was so secret.

As the dinner crowd started to build. Her mother, Mary, and Daisy, stopped into the diner on their way home from work. They didn't usually eat, but they often bought pies to take home since no one really had time to make them anymore.

Ruth met them at the counter. "Ma, do you want some berry pie?"

Mary smiled. "I do. But cut a piece off for Daisy to take home. We don't need the whole thing."

Ruth pulled a full pie from the case and cut a large slice for Daisy. "I heard some awful rumors about Mr. Orwell." Ruth whispered and nodded toward the table of gossipers.

"Mind your business, Ruth. Those old biddies should work more and talk less. We'll need every person we can get, and they'll be lucky to keep their job if people at the factory gets wind of it."

"Why do you need every person?" asked Ruth.

"We're going to be making combat boots." Daisy said. "Thousands of them."

Ruth wondered if Joe would be wearing a pair of boots made at the Orwell factory and then realized he probably already had his issue of shoes. "They said Mr. Orwell put his wife in an insane asylum. How can that be possible?"

"Ruth. I told you once. Mind your business. A man can have his wife committed, especially if he has lots of money. It's not right and not fair, but it is the law in this state."

"It's outrageous if you ask me," added Daisy.

"It is." Agreed Mary. "But we have our own families to worry about, so let's keep them front and center in our minds."

Ruth leaned in and whispered. "They said women are having affairs while their husbands are away."

Mary scowled. "For the love of Christ, girl." She hissed. "I'm fairly certain we didn't send a collection of altar boys to fight a war, and for the last time, mind your business. What if they were talking about Mae or Daisy or you, for that matter. How would you feel? This is hard enough for everyone without feeling you are being judged by a group of busybodies."

Ruth felt completely ashamed and packed up the pie. "I'm sorry Ma. I'll stick to my own business."

"Good. Now, how much is the pie?"

Ruth smiled. "It's on me. I'll use the tip from their table."

"You don't have to do that," Daisy said, reaching into her pocketbook.

"I want to. I eat here for free. You have others to feed. So please, it's on me."

Mary nodded, and Daisy thanked her. Ruth handed them their pie and grinned at Daisy. "Kiss my nieces for me."

Daisy returned the smile and said, "happily."

Ten

Melvin had regained much of his strength, but still had trouble eating. He had lost over fifty pounds and his once powerful frame was now more of a taut skeleton. Allison was working at the Moreland's house and some at the diner. Together, they made ends meet.

Mary had let him cut wood off from their land to generate some income, and he paid her a small percentage for a stumpage fee. He and Calvin had always cut softwoods like spruce and fir to send to the Monroe Paper Mill, but that was a volume business. Softwood paid less, but you were able to make up for it in volume and it was much easier to handle. On the farm there was not a lot of softwood. The acres owned by the McGinns were covered with maple, birch, ash and oak. Great for furniture and firewood, but much, much heavier, especially working alone. When Sean wasn't busy at the farm, he came and helped, but that was sporadic, so Melvin usually fell the trees and twitched them out one or two at a time with ponies.

He had a yard full of logs and was contemplating the best way to cut them. Eight-foot logs tended to be the preferred length at most sawmills, but they were nearly impossible to handle alone. The other hassle was that the chainsaw he and Calvin used was a two-man saw, dangerous and nearly impossible to man alone. If Sean wasn't available, he occasionally found a man looking for work hanging around the diner.

This morning was one of those days. He drove to the filling station for gas for the saw and found a group of men sitting at the diner counter drinking coffee.

Ruth was at the counter, and Melvin sat down. She brought him a glass of milk. He enjoyed coffee, but his stomach was still tender, and a hot cup of coffee was akin to pouring molten lava into his gut.

Ruth smiled. "We have blueberry muffins if you're interested."

"That would be nice," he said. "Did your sister make them?"

"One of them probably did. Why?" she asked with a crinkled brow.

"Allison's tend to be dry, that's all," he said with a deadpan expression.

Ruth inhaled deeply and grinned. "Oh, I'm telling her you said that. You should know not to question a McGinn woman's baking skills." Then laughed, shaking her head. "Tsk, tsk, tsk."

"I've told her that myself, and her biscuits aren't as fluffy as your mother's. I've told her that too."

Ruth laughed. "Ha! We've told her she's over-kneading the dough. But she never listens. I'll get you a moist muffin if I can find one." Then turned to the other end of the counter.

Melvin liked Ruth. She was a sweet girl with a big heart, and he really like Joe as well. In fact, he liked all the McGinns and sometimes wished he had met Allison first. He had never married and for a while he thought that Emma might be the one, but she was young, and he wasn't ready to settle down. She had made the best life for herself by marrying Bill Moreland, and he was happy for her.

Ruth returned with the muffin. It was cut in half and had been toasted on the griddle with a little butter. Just the way he liked it. He looked at the men sitting at the counter, eyeing them up to for who might want some work when the door opened, and he heard someone call his name.

"Melvin Carrigan. How the hell are you?"

He turned to and saw Tom Diamond. Tom was a trucker who often took the Carrigan's wood to the mill since they didn't have a large truck themselves. Tom was a large man in his fifties, with black hair and a long black beard that had always reminded Melvin of Paul Bunyan.

Melvin stood up and reached for Diamond's hand. "I'm hanging on Tom. You?"

"Busy. Always busy." Diamond sat down beside him and ordered a coffee. "Cuttin' much wood?"

Melvin nodded. "Yeah. Hardwood for furniture, but with the war on, there ain't much going on in the furniture business."

Tom nodded. "Yeah, they're still making paper in town, but they only have enough men for one machine and don't plan on looking for a crew for the other one until the war is over."

"Well, that's no good." Replied Melvin.

"No, I suppose not," Tom said and sipped his coffee. "How much wood do you have?"

Melvin stopped and pictured the wood yard in his mind. "Handy on to twenty cord I'd imagine. But the sawmills are only buying a little a time. I'll probably use what I can't sell for firewood. It will be winter before we know it."

"That's a fact. Is it already cut up?"

"No, it's tree length. I was just contemplating on that during the drive over here."

Diamond smiled. "Then I might have something you'd like. The old stick mill across the river in Ames is looking for bolt wood."

Melvin had never heard the term before and gave Diamond a puzzled look. "Bolt wood?"

"Yeah, that's what they call it. Forty inches long and they are particular about not being shorted. They are making gunstocks for rifles. They have to be at least six inches in diameter, too."

Melvin was a little energized and quickly did the math in his head. He figured maybe fifteen or sixteen cords of the pile would be over six inches and he could get five or six forty-inch sticks per tree. That would be a lot of gunstocks and what was left he would saw up for firewood.

"How do I get in on that?" Melvin said with a smile.

"I have tickets for about a hundred cords, and they'll be giving out more. I'm working with some other guys, but you and your brother have always been good to work with, so I'll take care of you first."

Melvin was flattered. "Jesus, Tom. Thank you so much. I can have it cut up by the end of the week. What will I owe you?"

"We'll do our usual hauling fee. Sounds fair?"

"Hell, yes, it's fair. Cal is somewhere fighting the war, so I'm working alone. I can help load, but this ulcer damn near killed me."

"Shit, don't worry about that. I have a crew of young guys working for me. In fact, if you need another man for the saw, I'll send one over."

Melvin couldn't believe his ears. He had been feeling low for a very long time after his illness, and he was starting to feel the blood running through his body again. "Yes. I can use a man."

Tom sipped his coffee and grinned. "They'll be sober too. I don't allow any drinking on my jobs. You'll appreciate that."

"Yes, I will." Melvin replied with deep satisfaction.

"Speaking of drinking. What branch did your idiot brother join?"

There was a time where that might have insulted Melvin, but that time was long gone. "We haven't seen him. He walked off at her wedding," nodding toward Ruth who was at the other end of the counter, "and haven't heard a word from him since. Someone told me he is in the Navy on a troop transport. Someone else said he had already been to the brig more than once for drunkenness."

Tom shook his head. "That sounds like him. I'm sorry, Melvin. Cal is a good worker when he's sober. The problem is... he never is."

"He came by it natural. Our father was the same way."

"You turned out fine," said Diamond.

"The difference was that I hated my father's drinking and Calvin idolized him. He never could see the difference."

Allison came home to find Melvin working in the yard and dripping with sweat. His shirt and pants were soaked through with perspiration.

She walked toward him with Jim and Alan toddling beside her. "My God Melvin. Be sure to drink some water," and as she neared him, she could smell him. "And please take a bath. It's hot enough already and you'll stink up the house." She said with a laugh.

Melvin smiled and picked up a gallon pail and drank from it. The water spilled round the corner of his mouth and dribbled down his shirt. Then he poured a little water over his head. "Ah. Refreshing. All clean."

Allison shook her head and stood with her hands on her hips. "I can still smell you."

Melvin shrugged. "Maybe it's you." He flicked the bucket forward and soaked the front of her linen shirt.

Allison stood in shock with her mouth open. But the coolness of the water felt good, and she started laughing. "You dirty sneak! I'll get you for that!"

As she flicked the water from her hands, Melvin saw that the wet shirt was clinging to her, and he saw her dark nipples through the cloth. When she flicked her hands, they jiggled lightly, and he felt a thrill. Then a bit ashamed and tried to look away, but he was seeing her differently for the first time. She was his brother's wife, but he wanted her. Intimately.

Allison pulled the shirt from her chest, releasing the fabric, and looked at Melvin. She realized that he had been staring at her breasts and blushed a little. "I'm going to make some dinner and I'll put some water on the stove for washing."

Melvin returned to his regular self and nodded. "Thanks. I'll be in soon." As she walked away, he noticed her hips, and that she had a woman's body now. No longer a child. He didn't know what to make of all these feelings, but he knew that he wanted her still.

That night after she had gone to bed, he laid on the couch and was thinking about her. Trying to recall the picture in his mind of the wet blouse and her supple hips. He was nearly asleep when he heard a creaking on the stairs. Allison was coming down as quietly as possible.

"Mel. Are you awake?" she whispered.

For a moment he thought of faking sleep, but he raised his head and whispered, "yes."

She walked to the bottom step and leaned over the railing. "Come to bed with me."

There was a long pause, and he felt himself filled with anxiety. "I don't know if that's a good idea."

"Why not? I know that you want to, and I do too."

He wanted to go badly, but he felt that he'd be in the wrong. "People might talk."

"I don't care. They probably do already with you living here."

He thought that was probably true. "What about Calvin?"

"Who?" she whispered.

He understood now that she had moved on with her life, and perhaps he should as well.

"I'm coming."

Eleven

M ae was working the night shift at Harland Hospital. She didn't mind it so much in the fall and winter, but the spring and summer made it hard to sleep during the day. What she liked most about it was that had had time to write to Finn. It was coming up on their anniversary and she wanted to send him something more than the usual report from home. Too many letters were small talk, like they had done every night at the dinner table, and he never really said where he was. Probably due to secrecy, but she knew that he was in the Pacific and all that she could imagine were palm trees and Hula girls in grass skirts, like in the movies.

She finished her rounds and sat down to start her message. The ward was only half-full, with so many men being away at war and Mae found herself missing Finn even more. She loaded her fountain pen started writing.

June 5' 1942

My dearest Finn

I can't believe that we have been married for a year now. It has been the best and yet hardest year of my life. The best because you are my husband and will be forever. I truly love you with all of my heart. The hardest because fate has pulled you away from me. But it only strengthens my resolve.

I dream about our life together when you get home. I want to have children as soon as you are ready. My greatest dream is to have a son that looks exactly like you to carry on the McGinn name. It's strange how the tragedy of losing young Alvin brought us together, but as soon as we had our first kiss, I knew you were the man I'd marry.

I am always impressed by your mother. She holds everyone together and is tough as nails. I feel bad for Sean because he is the last man standing in the house. Lord, help him.

No news from your brothers except that everything is well. Lewin will be home soon, and your mother says that no news is good news regarding the rest.

Before I say goodnight to you, I want to share a dream that I had last night. I dreamed that we were at the farm holding a baby girl. Everyone fawned over her, and your mother asked her name and just like we had discussed you said Mary and your mother wept. It was beautiful. I have never really put much belief in dreams, but that one was so real that I remember it like I was there in person.

This is the end-of-year one for us, of many and many. When we are old and gray, we can pull our letters out and read about what we were doing during the war. Come home safely, Finn. I stop in the chapel and ask God to keep you from harm. I want my Finn back with me, safe and sound.

With all of my heart, my mind, and my soul I love you.

Mae

Mae glanced around to see that no one was watching and pulled a lipstick from her pocket and coated her lips. She laid the letter across a clipboard and kissed the blank space at the bottom of the letter. Then she pulled a piece of ribbon that she had sprayed in her perfume and slid it into the fold of the letter. She carefully loaded the envelope and stamped it. It would be on its way in the morning. The rest of the shift. She wondered about where he was and how he was doing. Was he warm and dry on some tropical beach? She really couldn't picture anything except Hawaii.

Guadalcanal

Braaap, braaap. Pow, pow, pow. The shots flew over Finn's head and palm fronds fell all over him as the vegetation was disintegrating all around him. They were pinned down, and they needed to keep moving forward, and the only way was to silence the machine guns ahead of them. He looked to his right and to his left. All of the men in his squad were with him, and so far, no one was wounded.

When he was named squad leader, he had attempted to hand pick his entire squad. He always sought out ballplayers. Baseball players in particular. Catchers, pitchers and outfielders were his preference, because they could all throw hard. But instead of baseballs, it was grenades. He wanted strong men and not some city accountant who had the bad luck of being drafted into the Marines. He wanted tough guys and killers. His one exception was Freddy Dumond. He had come to like him and since he was from Maine too, Finn felt the need to keep him close. Freddy was tough, but he wasn't much of a pitcher.

"Second squad!" Roared Finn, "When they stop to reload those machine guns, I'm going to count one, two, three and on three throw a grenade at those guns! If we pop up all together, it will confuse these mother fuckers! Once you hear the grenades blow, we're going over this berm. God help you if you don't go, because I'll come back here and deal with you personally! Understand?!"

He got nods and thumbs up from both sides.

"Ready grenades! Remember, no one here is allowed to die for their country. But let's make these sons of whores die for theirs!" At that, the men smiled and chuckled a little. There was a noticeable lull in firing and definitely no machine gun fire. "One! Two! Thrreeeee!" he screamed in rapid succession.

In one instant, a dozen men rose, threw simultaneous grenades and disappeared again. The grenades went off in a ragged chorus of explosions and a second after the last grenade,

Finn screamed at his team. "Go! Go you salty sons of bitches! Finish them!"

The squad poured over the berm and Finn heard sporadic gunfire, then saw a man drop to his right. He felt the rush of a bullet as it whizzed by less than an inch from his right cheek. There were dead Japs ahead of him and he focused hard on finding the living ones.

The Japanese manning the machine guns were dead and one gun was completely blown apart. Someone had scored a direct hit. Finn saw two Japanese soldiers trying to run, and he opened fire. The first soldier was dropped with that first shot, but the second one kept running. He emptied his clip and still the soldier was running down a path into a large gully. They were giving up the high ground.

Finn loaded a new clip into his M-1 rifle. He stopped and aimed carefully. He took a deep breath and held it for a beat, then squeezed the trigger. I second later he saw the man's helmet go flying and his head explode in a spray of blood and brains.

The enemy fire had stopped, and he heard the groans of wounded men around him. Get the weapons away from those prisoners and set up a line to protect our front and flanks.

One of the men is his squad was an American of half Japanese descent named Reese. His Father was white, his mother Japanese and Reese was fluent in both languages.

Finn yelled, "Get private Reese up here!" and a chorus of "Reese, Reese," went down the line. He noticed Dumond staring at him wide eyed and catching his breath.

"Corporal, two men down. Ellis is dead and Lafferty took a bullet through the shoulder."

Finn nodded and tried to think of his next order. "Freddy. Get a couple of guys and get Lafferty to the aid station and have someone make a litter and take Ellis' body back."

Freddy nodded and immediately took off to find help. Finn was Corporal, and he waited for their platoon leader Lieutenant, Schwartz, before issuing any further commands. The men were searching the dead Japanese and had three wounded men tied together and a fourth man was tied to the rest of them without a scratch.

Finn studied him curiously. *Lucky SOB I guess*, he thought.

A stocky farmer from North Carolina named Wiggins approached Finn. "This one here was playin' dead." He said, pointing at the unharmed man. "He's a goll-dang coward."

Finn looked at the man again and when his eyes met Finn's he dropped his head and stared at the ground.

"Coward, huh. Every unit's got some."

The man cleared his throat. "I am not a coward."

Finn and Wiggins were stunned. He spoke English without much of an accent at all.

"You speak English?" asked Finn.

"Yes. I'm from San Francisco." He replied and dropped his head again.

"Why are you here, then?" asked Wiggins.

"Family honor. My father sent me back to Japan before the attack on Pearl Harbor and I am doing my family honor."

"Yeah. Well, you gonna' die for the Emperor boy, I promise you that."

Finn turned to Wiggins. "Go find out what's holding Reese up." Wiggins nodded and left.

Reese came bounding up the trail breathless. "Sorry Corporal, I was down on the far end, and I have these." He handed a packet of documents to Finn. "Letters mostly, some others that seem to be in code and a couple of maps. One looks like this ridge and across the valley looks like a similar set-up with machine-gun nests or maybe a couple *pill-boxes*. I can't tell."

"Thanks Reese. See if you can get anything out of these guys," and Pointed at the prisoners.

Reese began questioning them in Japanese, and the uninjured man refused to speak either English or Japanese. After a few minutes of questioning, Lt. Schwartz and Sargent Metzger came up the hill with reinforcements.

"Nice work McGinn," Schwartz said, looking at all the dead Japanese. "Are the two we passed on the trail our only casualties?"

"Yes, sir." Finn replied.

"What's this?" asked Schwartz, pointing at the prisoners.

"We're trying to get info out of them."

Reese stood up and turned to Schwartz. "They said that there are about two-hundred men on the ridge across from us."

Metzger whistled. "Wow. That's a lot of Japs."

Schwartz was fresh from West Point and had a command presence like the Academy officers often did. "Sargent Metzger, get our reinforcements up here and send for more ammo and grenades. Let's keep our line fairly tight so they can't come through us, but not so tight that we get flanked."

"Yes, sir." Metzger replied and started barking orders to everyone around.

"What do you want to do with these prisoners, sir?"

Schwartz looked over at the four Japanese men. Two were on the verge of death. He sighed. "Orders are no prisoners. We have no way to guard them and nothing to feed them. We can barely feed ourselves and we're moving forward in the morning."

Finn's heart sunk. They were told that the Japanese were not taking prisoners either, so they were told to fight to the death. But this wasn't a fight, this was slaughter. "Yes, sir," he said and pulled his .45 caliber pistol from its holster. he paused trying to reconcile his mind.

"You can order your men to do it you know," added Schwartz.

Finn stared at him with impassive eyes and cocked the pistol. "I know."

He raised the pistol and pointed at the man that was closest to death. Finn figured that he had suffered the longest.

"Kill me first," said the English speaker, and he locked eyes with Finn, refusing to blink. Finn pointed the gun at the man's forehead. The man's face turned from one of defeat to one of defiance. Finn squeezed the trigger and the Japanese soldier's head snapped back and he fell in a heap. The others started screaming in what Finn assumed was prayers and one by one he silenced them. When he re-holstered his weapon, he turned and saw Schwartz actually grinning.

"Well done Corporal." He said, and his grin turned into a smile. "Well done indeed."

Finn didn't return the smile and stood at attention. "If there's nothing else, sir. I'd like to see that my men are properly positioned."

"Of course. See to it." Finn walked past him, and all the men around were staring at him.

Reese walked next to him and whispered. "You okay?"

Finn paused and decided not to answer that question. "What were they saying before I shot them?"

Reese shrugged and said, "they were calling for their mothers."

"Go see to your position. We attack in the morning, but I suspect they'll be here tonight."

Reese nodded, "Aye-aye," and started to walk away.

"Belay that. Move your position next to me. I want you nearby in case we need to figure out what they are saying."

Reese nodded again and headed over the berm.

Finn walked into the woods and when he was alone. He vomited and sat on a log. He felt the hot sting of tears as he thought about his own mother and wondered if he would call her name or Mae's when his time came.

Twelve

Lewin sat on the edge of his bed, looking at his withered right leg in amazement. It was like a skeleton leg from some Halloween decoration. His left leg looked powerful from all the weeks of walking on crutches. Like something carved in a statue. The hospital ward was quiet, and most of the men were still asleep. He reached under his pillow and pulled out a bundle of letters and pictures neatly folded into a packet. On top was his discharge letter from the Army. He was going home.

He studied it with mixed emotions. He was happy to be going home to his family, but also had a feeling of guilt. He was injured in an accident, but he never went to war. So many men were dying overseas every day, and he was going home with shrapnel from a faulty oven.

It weighed on him greatly, and he wondered if he had done his part. At the time of the accident, he was being reprimanded for being a sloppy soldier. He doubted that Finn or Joe Roy was ever reprimanded for that. Even Alder, who wasn't a much of a fighter, was probably a good soldier. It seemed that everyone in his platoon had done a round on KP, so maybe the Sargent was just looking for someone to send. He'd never know and felt pretty bad.

His sullen mood was lifted when he heard a bustle at the end of the ward that meant the change of shift for the medical staff. He leaned to look down the long space between the rows of beds and saw Armstrong bounding toward him with a big smile. It filled Lewin's heart with joy.

"Mr. McGinn," he said with his hand extended.

Lewin smiled back. "Mr. Armstrong," and gripped his hand and shook it.

"This is it for you. Home by nightfall. I'm a jealous man," he said with a laugh.

Lewin's expression saddened a little. "I can't believe it. I'm happy to be going home, but I feel that. I just..." he struggled to find the words.

Armstrong smiled at him and tried to lighten his mood. "You just gonna' miss me?"

That made Lewin chuckle for a second. "Yes, I am going to miss you. You've been my best friend in the Army." Then he saddened again. "I just wanted to do my part. I don't know that I did."

Armstrong put his hand on Lewin's shoulder. "Look at me."

Lewin saw that Armstrong had a sincere look in his eyes. "We all do what we do. Do you think I want to fetch bedpans and wipe asses? I joined the Army to be a soldier, not a house slave.

93

But they don't want me for that." He paused in thought and studied Lewin's face. "I can shoot as good as any man in North Carolina. I've hunted my whole life and I've fought my whole life. But they got me doing this. So, I do it." He took a breath and exhaled. "When I was a boy, my father told me it don't matter what you decide to do in life, but whatever you decide, do it well. So, I swallowed my pride, and I swallowed my anger, and I do this. And I try hard to do it well. So that my father would be proud of me."

Lewin felt a bit foolish now. Like a whining child who didn't get his way. "You're the best. One of the best men I have ever met, and I appreciate all you've done for me. Your father would be proud."

Armstrong nodded and appreciated the sentiment. "Thank you, Lewin."

"No, thank you Amos. I'll never forget all you've done for me."

Amos smiled and shook Lewin's hand again. They didn't need to speak anymore; the respect was mutual. Then Amos went about his duties. Half an hour later, he returned.

He turned to Lewin with a broad, toothy smile. "Your chariot has arrived. Time to go home."

Home. Lewin's heart pounded at the word, and he drove his crutches into the floor to stand.

"Easy now. I don't want you to fall and break that leg again. You'll be spending the fall with me."

Lewin held out a hand, and Armstrong helped him to his feet. "Thanks again Amos. When this is over, come to Maine and visit us if you can. You're always welcome in a McGinn house."

Amos patted him on the back. "I might just do that. But not in January," he said with a laugh.

"Wise man," replied Lewin.

Amos helped him across the ward and out into the yard where a car was waiting. Lewin felt the sun on his face, and it felt good. It felt like days when he worked his garden, and that made him happy. "They'll take you from here. Good luck."

Lewin slid into the car and rolled down the window to say goodbye. He waved and Amos waved back, then started in with his Amos Jones routine. "Oh Lordy, they's gotta be many a bedpan that needs rinsin'! A man's work is never done!"

This made Lewin laugh and Amos turned back, smiling with one more wave.

As they drove through the gates past the last sentry, Lewin felt an odd sense of relief. He was out and soon he'd be back home with his wife and children. He could feel tears starting to sting his eyes and he wondered if it was the joy of going home or the fact that his time in the Army was over. Maybe it was some of both.

Cecelia paced nervously across the kitchen floor. It was nearly dinnertime, and she had expected him an hour earlier. The house was clean, and the children were dressed in their Sunday best. Mary held the baby Ernest, and Frances was playing dolls with Ellie.

Mary smiled at Cecelia. "Come on now, dear. You're going to wear a path in the floor and Lewin will have to sand it out. Come sit. Take some tea."

"I'm sorry Ma. I just... I think I might burst if I don't see him soon."

Mary looked her up and down. "I think that's true," she said with a chuckle.

Cecelia took a deep breath. "I think I will make some tea. Let me put some water on to boil."

She stood at the slate sink and pumped the log handle of the hand pump and water began to flow. She moved the cast-iron kettle under the running water and started to fill it when she heard the faintest sound of a car engine and saw the Moreland farm truck coming with a long cloud of dust rising up behind it.

She screamed and startled everyone, waking the baby.

"My god, woman. Get ahold of yourself," Mary chided.

"He's HOME!" she yelled and ran to the door. Flung it open and stood, barely able to breathe. The few minutes it took for the truck to drive down the road seemed like an eternity. She felt a little lightheaded and then gasped a huge breath. In her excitement, she had forgotten to breathe. Mary, Frances, and the children joined her on the porch and Frances was squeezing Ellie so tightly that Ellie complained. "Auntie Frannie, you hurting me." Frances loosened her grip and kissed her on the cheek.

The truck turned into the driveway, and they could see Lewin and Wishe with smiles on their faces. It was a shock to Mary to see Wishe smiling. But then again, he knew the feeling of coming home.

The truck stopped and Cecelia bolted to the door and whipped it open. Lewin tried to get his crutches stabilized when she pulled him bodily from the truck and squeezed him. She wept and wept. Then he held her back and kissed her face over and over. Then his own tears fell, and he was finally home.

A moment later, Frances released Ellie, and she ran to him. She was beautiful in her Sunday dress and ran with her arms outstretched and her wild red curls flopping in the air. He thought for a moment about kneeling to meet her, but as soon as he flexed his right leg a pain shot through his knee, and he winced.

She flung her little arms around his left leg and squeezed. "Daddy, we missed you so much."

He reached down and picked her up and kissed her cheek. She wrapped her arms around his neck and squeezed and he loved the feel of her soft curly hair on his face.

Mary stepped up and kissed his cheek. "Welcome home, son. There's someone else who wants to say hello." She handed Ernest to him, and Lewin smiled.

"I missed you all so much," in a hoarse croak, as his voice was raw with emotion.

Cecelia wiped her eyes and straightened her blouse. Come inside. I have dinner all ready. "Wishe will you please eat with us?" she asked.

Wishe stood silently for a moment then shook his head. "I can't. This is a time for family."

Mary gave him a reproachful look. "Nonsense. You are family to me. Come inside and I won't be refused."

Wishe shot a look at Lewin.

"You'd better come eat," Lewin said with a smile.

Everyone in the family said that Wishe was not afraid of any man, but every man was afraid of Mary.

"What's for dinner?" Lewin asked.

"Pea soup with lots of ham," Cecelia said.

"Is it thick how I like it?" he said with a smile.

"You can stand a spoon in it yourself if you want."

Lewin smiled with satisfaction.

The dinner was excellent and after everyone had left, he sat on the couch with Cecelia leaning on one shoulder and Ellie asleep beside him while he held Ernest. He thought about the Army and Amos and decided. This is where his duty was. He was home.

Thirteen

December 1942

It was dark so early in December in Maine. At least there were enough clouds in the sky to keep a little humidity in the air. Somehow, thirty-degree weather felt better with a little humidity. It didn't do much for visibility though, and Sean had his lantern as bright as he could get it so that neither of them would break their neck on the frozen muck.

The McGinn's closest neighbors the Hartley's were having a barn dance at their farm and all the young people in the area would be there. It was strange to go to dances without many adults, but since most of the men were away, only the teenagers still came out.

Lillian loved the Hartley girls. They were around her age, and they were always happy. She had never seen them be mean to anyone. She noticed that the older she got, the *cattier* the local girls were. She thought maybe it was because there were so few men around.

Lillian touched her hair, "I'm glad it's not too cold. I didn't want to wear a hat."

Sean snickered and adjusted his fedora. "Men can wear a hat, and no one cares. A woman wears a hat, and it's the end of the world."

"We take time to make ourselves look nice. You should appreciate that. What if we all started smearing bear fat in our hair like you? That wouldn't be very attractive."

"I don't use bear fat anymore. I have Murray's pomade. It's the best, and if you did use it, it would save a lot of time." He laughed aloud at his own wit.

Lillian plunged her hands into her pockets in an effort to keep them warm. "No woman will ever want you. You're too unrefined, and a doofus like you is a dime a dozen in town."

"Well. We aren't in town, are we?" He chuckled again.

They walked along, watching the road for anything that would trip them up in the dark. December was an odd time. The days sometimes got above freezing, making the roads soft and then frozen again when the sun went down, making them treacherous.

Sean reached over and took her by her upper arm. "Watch your step Lil. It's icy through here and you don't want to fall." He held the light between them to help light their way.

Lillian smiled and thought, *there may just be hope for this boy yet*.

They could see the Hartley farm in the distance, and they could hear the music and people talking.

"This is going to be fun," he said. "Sounds like a lot of people."

As they rounded the small snowbank at the edge of the Hartley farm, they saw the doors wide open and a fire burning in the driveway. Lillian smiled. "I'm finding my friends."

Sean snickered. "I'm finding a drink."

"No fighting Sean. Ma said."

"Don't be a snitch Lil."

"I'm not a snitch. Ma said no fighting and she'll know."

Sean chuckled to himself and realized that she would know. She always did. He decided that tonight it would be better to be a lover than a fighter. He started to the bonfire when he heard his name.

"Sean McGinn! Come here, son!"

He looked up to see Cy Hartley. He was sitting in a chair on his porch with a bear skin draped over his shoulders. His face was gaunt, but the skin made him appear like some great king.

Sean approached the porch with a broad smile. He liked Cy Hartley because he always told him stories of his father Alvin. He only believed half of them, but they were fun to listen to. "Evenin' Mr. Hartley."

"Does your mother let you drink whiskey?" Cy said with a wry smile.

"She would prefer not, but she doesn't fuss much about it when I do."

Cy smiled. "Good, come here son and sit with me for a few minutes. We'll share a little whiskey and I'll tell you a story about your Da."

Sean wanted to see what girls were here, but he liked Cy and he liked Whiskey. "Yes sir." Sean sat in the chair beside Cy.

Cy pulled a bottle out from under the skin and pointed to a cup on the little table that sat between them. Sean picked it up and Cy began to pour. At first, he expected a small drink, but Cy kept pouring and Sean's eyes grew bigger. When he stopped pouring, he stared at the cup in astonishment.

"I call that a Finn pour."

"A Finn pour? Like my brother Finn?"

Cy grinned through a mouth with no teeth. "Yes, one and the same. That boy can drink. So, I'll give you a Finn pour. I'm stuck here with my wife and daughters and no men to talk with. I appreciate the company so you'll drink a little and sit with me."

Sean sipped the whiskey, and the smokey flavor burned his throat. Then seemed to warm him. "That's a great skin. Did you shoot that bear?"

Cy ran his eyes over it, smiling. "Yes, I did. That's the story that I wanted to tell you about your Da. I thought of it when I grabbed this old skin."

Sean sipped his whiskey and listened intently.

"We were hunting on the back side of Howell Mountain over in Sparta." Cy sipped his own whiskey. "We were actually deer hunting when we heard branches snapping and a grunting coming through the trees in this little valley. I saw him first and

103

pulled up and shot. Hit that big SOB right in the forehead and he dropped." He sipped again. "Your father was already in the valley and was walking up to it to finish it off."

Cy paused and grinned, taking a long drink. "He leaned his rifle against a tree and squatted to check out the bear. Just as he leaned to see my handy work, the bear came too and roared. Then it struggled to get to its feet. Your father took off like he was shot out of a damn cannon. He grabbed his gun and started firing wildly, behind him."

Sean laughed. "Holy shit. He must have been scared."

"Oh, he was. It jumped me too. I pulled up and put three shots into the bear's ribs and he went down in a heap. This time he was dead." Cy chuckled, "When I got down there, your father was coming back. He stopped and took off his pants. He took off his long-johns and finished wiping the shit from his ass and chucked the long-johns in the woods! Ha-ha!"

"He shit his own pants?" Sean asked in astonishment.

"He did. He didn't fill em', but he couldn't wear them home in the state they were in."

"Wow. He never told us that story."

"I've never spoken of it again, not even to him, until just now. Not to anyone. He was my friend and when I saw this old skin, it reminded me of him. I miss him. I miss your uncle Kevin too. They were good men. Real good."

"I honestly never knew either one of them. Kevin was dead long before I was born and sometimes, I think that I can remember my father, but I was barely two when he died, so I know I'm just trying to convince myself."

"That's why I like to tell you those stories. So, you'll know."

"Thanks Mr. Hartley."

Cy chuckled. "Christ, son, we're drinking whiskey together. Call me Cy."

"Okay thanks, Cy."

"Oh. I had a question. How are you folks set on hens? A fox got into the chickens and killed damn near all my hens. I got him and I'll be wearing him someday too. But now we could use some layers."

Sean smiled. "Now that's something we have in abundance. Lillian is obsessed with winning chick prizes at the fair, so we keep most of the chicks. I could send you half a dozen if you want. That would save having to feed them."

Cy reached out and patted Sean on the forearm. "I'd be grateful. I can pay you for them."

Sean held up his hand. "Someday a fox might get into ours and you can return the favor."

Cy smiled at Sean and his eyes seemed a little watery. "Sean, you looked and sounded *exactly* like Alvin there."

"Really?" That made Sean smile.

"You done that whiskey?"

Sean brough the cup to his lips and drank down the remaining swallow. "I am now."

"Go have fun. Dance with a girl."

Sean grinned. "Thanks. I will." I jumped up and headed down the steps.

"Sean!"

He stopped and turned to Cy.

"No fighting. Your mother will know."

Sean laughed aloud and headed toward the fire. As he warmed himself, Lillian and the Hartley sisters came to the fire with a girl he didn't recognize. She was beautiful. She had ash brown hair and green eyes. Her complexion was milky white except for her cheeks and nose that were red from the cold. He couldn't take his eyes off her. Her face appeared young, but she had developed something of a woman's body. She had full lips, and he was imagining what it might be like to kiss them.

"Sean. It's not polite to stare!" shouted Lillian from across the fire, and the four girls all laughed.

He could feel his face flush with embarrassment. "I was thinkin' about something, that's all."

The girl smiled. "About asking me to dance? This is a barn dance, after all."

Sean stood up straight and puffed his chest a bit. "Yes, I was." He walked around the fire and held out his hand. "That's exactly what I was thinking about." When she took his hand, he nearly melted. She had delicate, small hands like something you'd see on a China doll.

The song was ending, and a new song started. It was *Stardust*. A slow song. Sean found the clarinet songs annoying, but he was happy to be waltzing with this girl.

He stared into her eyes. They were hard to see in the low light of the barn, but somehow, he could still see the green. "What's your name?"

She smiled sheepishly, "Harriett Cyr. I'm a cousin of the Hartley's."

"How come I never seen you before?"

She stood on her toes. "Because I live way at the tippy top of Maine." She lost balance and fell into him with a giggle.

He caught her and pulled her close. "You almost fell."

"I knew you would catch me."

"How did you know?"

"Because my cousins said that the McGinns are the best men in the county." Sean suddenly realized that she must have had a couple of drinks. He liked that.

"Well, my brothers are good men, but I have yet to prove myself."

She pulled back to look into his eyes and frowned. "Don't be silly. You just did. You saved a young lady in distress. My hero!" She laughed. Leaned in and kissed him on the mouth.

Her lips were everything that he had imagined, and he kissed her back.

Fourteen

January 1, 1943

The Narwhal had been in port at the Mare Island Shipyard in Vallejo, California since late September. She was being refitted with new torpedo tubes, torpedo storage, batteries and engines. Patrick was was responsible for seeing that not only were the tubes installed correctly, but that the men understood the new processes for handling torpedoes. The one part of this assignment that he liked was liberty passes and Chief Halpert was extremely generous in handing them out. They had been at sea almost non-stop for the past year ever since the attack on Pearl, they were perpetually hunting Japanese shipping.

When they arrived in California, he was hoping for a leave to visit home, but that wasn't possible. However, he was able to call, and he made the most of it. He called the farm at a pre-arranged time to have as much of his family there, ready to talk. Today, he decided to skip the phone call however, he was on a weekend pass in San Francisco. His hotel was just above fisherman's wharf and overlooked Alcatraz. It intrigued him that Al Capone, "Machine Gun" Kelly and "Creepy" Karpis were all there as inmates. *So many bad guys in one space, that must be a preview of hell*, he thought.

Patrick rode the cable car a while. He didn't care about the destination, he just enjoyed seeing the sights. The men on the Narwhal had come back from their passes, raving about the food in Chinatown, so when he heard the trolley driver call out for that stop, he hopped off and started walking around. This place was like nothing like he had ever seen in his life. He walked into the neighborhood under an arch that spanned the entire street. Lions and dragons were painted everywhere and food stalls, clothing stores lined both sides of the street. The smells were both awful and alluring all at the same time.

Patrick was drawn to a stall with rusty metal tubs packed with live fish, including octopus. He had never seen a live octopus before and had never eaten one. It was coiled up in the bottom of the tub, he started to feel a little curious about what they might taste like. He was about to ask a question of the stall owner when a conversation broke out in Chinese beside him. The vendor and another man were haggling about the price and when they had agreed, fish monger reached into a bamboo tube and pulled out a short metal spear with a trident on the end. He loomed over the tub and continued to speak to the customer in Chinese. His eyes moved with the motion of the fish and when he had locked on the target, he flicked his wrist and the spear pierced the water like a flash to skewer a fish. The fish came out of the water thrashing wildly and the man pinned it to a cutting board with his left hand and took its head off with a blow from a cleaver in his right. Then he ran the blade down the middle of the fish, flipped it over and did it again, creating two of the best filets Patrick had ever seen. He was a master with the cleaver. He repeated this with a couple more fish from the tub and tossed the spent carcasses into a bucket at the back of his stall.

That explains the stink, thought Patrick. Each time the man tossed a piece of old fish into it, a swarm of flies would emerge and then quickly return to their places. His attention was distracted by a new smell and the sizzle of vegetables in a wok. He wandered to that stall and watched. The cook moved quick as a flash, adding vegetables and spices. Then tossing the contents in his hand like he had seen people flip pancakes back home. He was mesmerized.

"Hoy, sailor. You come eat."

Patrick turned to see a slightly built Chinese man smiling at him.

"Oh...ah I don't know. I have never..." The man smiled and grabbed Patrick by the arm, tugging him toward a table. For January, it was unseasonably warm, so he decided to eat outside.

"I give you big meal. You kill Japs? Yes?"

Patrick wasn't sure what to make of him, but nodded yes.

"Very good. I give you A-number-one deal. One dollar."

"I'm not sure what to order," Patrick said, staring at a menu of words he had never heard or seen before.

The man smiled and nodded, "you kill Japs. I take care of you."

Patrick knew the stories of Japanese atrocities on the Chinese people and apparently this man did as well.

"One dollar. Okay?" he persisted.

"Sure. Okay."

The man clapped his hands and started shouting in Chinese. A moment later, a young woman in a red silk shirt came out holding a pot with a thick cloth. She poured some tea into an ornate cup with Chinese writing.

Patrick lifted the tea and smiled. He went to sip and jumped as he burned his lip on the hot tea. The girl cringed and began speaking rapidly in Chinese and the friendly man, was no longer friendly yelled at her and she disappeared.

"So sorry. The tea is hot. Did you burn your mouth?"

"I'm fine. Is she okay?"

The man was confused. "Is who okay?"

Patrick pointed inside. "That girl that gave me the tea."

"Yes. She's fine. She'll bring soup soon. Do you like a spicy soup or no spices?"

Patrick was apprehensive. He didn't like seeing her yelled at. He tried to imagine if someone yelled at one of his sisters like that at the diner. It made him uncomfortable. "Not spicy, I guess."

"Okay, yes. Very good," and he began yelling in Chinese again.

Then the same girl came with a bowl and placed it on the table along with the funniest spoon Patrick had ever seen. The bowl and the spoon had the same writing on it.

She placed the bowl on the table and made a deep bow. "Please sir. I am so sorry. The soup is hot."

Patrick was a little surprised at how well she spoke English was, and as she turned, he called out. "Excuse me?"

She turned shyly and Patrick smiled. "What does this writing say on the cups and bowls?"

It is the story of our family. It tells that we are from Nanning in the Sichuan province, and we are a family of fishermen on the Yong Jiang River. We have fished that river for ten generations."

"Ten generations? Holy smokes, how do they know that? How long ago is that?"

She giggled a little. "It may not be the same in English, but that is how it sounds translated. But we had been there for more than one-hundred years until the Japanese invaded. We took our belongings as far south as we could go, then sold everything to take a boat to America."

The man interrupted again in Chinese, but in a much softer tone, and she bowed and returned inside.

"This is egg flower soup. You try it. Like mother's chicken noodle, only no chicken yet, just egg." At this bit of wit, he burst out laughing and Patrick couldn't help but to laugh as well.

He tried the soup. It had cooled to a pleasant temperature, and it tasted like heaven. It was a chicken broth with egg floating in it, along with some chopped green onion and some other spice that he couldn't place. In fact, he couldn't place more than a few spices in the dish, but they gave him a warm feeling and he tore through the bowl and drained the broth.

"You like it yes?" asked the Chinese man.

"Yes, I did. Very much. What is your name?"

The man smiled and nodded. "You call me Yan."

"Thank you, Yan."

The next course was small appetizers of shrimp steamed in dough. The flavors were a revelation as well. It came with a salty dark sauce filled with chives and tiny bits of ginger. He had eaten meat and potatoes for nearly every meal of his life, and this was like being taken to another planet.

The main course was chicken fried with vegetables and peanuts over noodles. This was spicier than the previous dishes, but it warmed warmed him to his core. He ate every morsel and when they tried to offer dessert, he leaned back this his hands up in the universal signal of surrender.

"I cannot eat another bite. Everything was delicious." He said with a smile as he patted his taut stomach.

"Okay, okay. I'm glad you like it. One dollar." Yan said with a grin, holding up his index finger.

Patrick knew that he had four dollars in his coat pocket and pulled out the folded bills, handing them to Yan.

Yan counted the bills and started shaking his head. Pulling three out and he was about to hand them back when Patrick closed his hand around the bills. "Those are for you and the girl," he said, pointing inside.

Yan paused for a moment and then he understood. He smiled and nodded. "Li. Li. Her name is Li. My sister." Yan said, patting his chest.

"Well Yan, thank you for a lovely meal and a memorable afternoon."

Yan smiled and bowed over and over. As Patrick started to walk away, Yan grabbed him by the sleeve. Patrick turned and Yan handed him one of the intricately painted teacups. Patted his chest again and closed Patrick's hand around the cup and said, "Yan," one last time.

Patrick slipped the cup into his pocket and walked for an hour to work off his meal. He found that if he didn't stay active after a big meal, he would become sleepy and he had too much to see to be sleeping now.

As he walked, he was amazed by all of the tall buildings. *How do they not fall over?* He wondered. After an hour of walking, he grabbed another cable car and rode around the city for most of the day thinking about his brothers.

When he returned to his room, he sat down to write a letter to Jolene Jewell. He enjoyed writing to Jolene, and he liked hearing news from home, but he wanted someone to write to that was his and his alone. Her fiancé was a second lieutenant, in an infantry company somewhere in Europe. Patrick didn't wish him ill, but he really didn't care to hear about his exploits in letter after letter.

The next morning he walked to a Catholic Church he saw in his travels. Mass was just starting and hurriedly grabbed a seat.

He tended not to listen to the homilies of the priest and instead have private prayer with God. He always felt like he knew what he should be doing, so he didn't need a priest to spell it out for him. He prayed for his mother and siblings. The guys on the boat. A swift end to the war, and he felt a bit selfish about it, but he prayed for a woman of his own to write to.

While he was waiting to take communion, he walked up the aisle behind a long line of parishioners. He was still in thought as people passed him and he was shocked when Li walked by him and smiled. Then Yan came behind her and smiling and nodding. He was excited to see her and all of a sudden, he felt very hungry.

After the service. He spent the day in Chinatown eating and talking with his new friends.

Fifteen

The jungle on Guadalcanal was so thick that it put the deep Maine woods to shame. Finn scanned the sky, trying to gauge the sun versus the terrain, but the vegetation blocked his view in every possible direction. The bugs were thick, the rain was heavy, and the disease was killing his team. Of his original twenty-four, he was down to eight. Six were killed or wounded and ten fell victim to dysentery and jungle rot.

Wiggins was a big guy but didn't mind the heat being from the heart of North Carolina. The problem was that he was being knee deep in water day in and day out. The platoon tried to dry their socks when they could, but the rain made it impossible. It was a sunny day in December just before Christmas when Wiggins had removed his boots to try to dry them. He had been wearing them for more than a month without a good chance to dry them.

The socks were covered in green slime that resembled algae and when he removed them, his skin came off with them. His right foot was so macerated they could see a thin layer of muscle that covered the tendons that let him flex. His feet were like something out of a horror movie, like a half revealed mummy. The smell was like rotten cheese, and everyone had come to know the signs of gangrene.

Finn looked Wiggins in the eyes. "Jesus Billy Ray. That ain't good."

Wiggins tried touching the flesh. "They hurt like hell, Mac."

Finn turned and yelled, "pass the word for Doc Clinton!"

A minute later a Clinton came running up out of breath with his bag of first aid supplies. He stopped short when he saw Wiggins. He tore open a pouch of sulfur and poured it all over Wiggin's feet and then he added another. "Good Lord Wiggins. This is bad. I could smell the rot from five feet away."

Clinton glanced around at the other guys. "Everyone, get your boots and socks off! Keep your feet dry or you'll lose em'."

Wiggins popped up and frowned. "You think I'm gong to lose my foot Doc?"

Clinton stopped trying to treat it and met his gaze. "Yes. You're gonna' lose your right foot. I'm hopeful of saving the left though. You'll be going home if we can get you off from this island."

Wiggins grew angry and snatched at his boot then slid it on over his foot. "I'm not going home without all y'all. We're brothers."

Finn walked over and pulled him to his feet. When he bore the full weight of his body on his foot, he winced, and his eyes welled with tears as he fought back the pain. Then he let the tears flow as he realized that he couldn't walk ten more feet, let alone fight in combat. Finn made a motion to the other guys and tossed his head in a way that said, *disappear*, without words. He helped Wiggins back to the ground and handed him a canteen. "Let the doc get you out of here. You can go home and someday I'll come down there and you can take me catfishin' on the Neuse River that you're always talking about."

Wiggins laughed. "They don't let Yankees fish that river, son."

"People from Maine ain't Yankees. We hate city people from Massachusetts and New York too. Besides, if you went to Florida and kept travelin' south far enough, eventually you'd come back around hit Maine, so in truth, we're just deep, deep south."

Wiggins thought about that for a moment and burst into a laugh. "You're a good man McGinn. I would have died for you."

Finn gripped his hand and pulled him in. He was choked up by the sentiment and croaked in a hoarse whisper, "I know. Same here. I'm just glad you never had to." He paused for a long moment. "Semper Fi."

Wiggins patted him on the shoulder and nodded. "Semper Fi."

That evening Colonel Pearson briefed the officers on the assault planned for dawn. Their platoon was the to be the tip of the spear and assault the eastern side of the ridge and elements of the 3rd Marines would assault from the north. The southern slope was a vertical drop of eighty feet or so leaving only a western retreat for the Japanese and the Army had a company moving in a wide arc around the ridge to catch them on the run.

The plan made sense to Finn. The sooner they drove the Japs from the island, the sooner they could get some relief. As he walked along the path back to his platoon, he heard someone call his name.

"Finn! Finn McGinn!"

He turned to see John Roy coming toward him with a huge smile.

Finn stepped up and hugged him "You son of a bitch. I figured they killed you by now."

John laughed. "Ha-ha I can't be killed. I was dead once already when I drowned, and they brought me back to life."

"So, you're doing alright?" Finn said with a smile.

"Well, to tell the truth. I may be bulletproof, but this jungle rot is threatening to eat my balls," he said and scrunched up his face in torment as he scratched at his crotch.

Finn shook his head. "That's got to be a distraction."

John smiled. "Nah. Once the shootin' starts, I don't think about anything but killing. It's strange. I'm not a violent guy, but I hate these little sons of whores. I hate em' to my core."

"I ain't no particular fan myself. I figure the more we kill the faster we'll be home."

"Amen, brother," John said as he made the sign of the cross. "Hey where are you in this attack?"

"Eastern point of the spear, you?"

John reached out and shook Finn's hand hard. "Tip of the northern spear. Whichever one of us gets there last pays for a bottle of whiskey when we get leave again?"

Finn smiled. "Oh, hell yes. That's a deal worth fighting for."

The night was uneventful. Everyone expected a night attack, but none came. It was psychological warfare at its best. They had beaten back fourteen night attacks since August and now no one slept well for fear of being murdered in their foxhole.

Finn moved from hole to hole, getting his men ready. He had checked his own weapons three times already and was about to do a fourth when the Colonel's runner came hurrying up the line. "Pearson says start moving as quiet as you can up the ridge at 0530 and if you meet resistance deal with it. When the shooting starts, both spears will be coming fast."

Finn nodded. "Got it," he said, and the runner started further on down the line. Finn studied the men to his right and started giving hand signals, then repeated them to the men on the left. They had already been through two officers as platoon leader, but after the second one was killed, Finn was made platoon Sergeant.

He checked his weapons and ammo one last time and gave the signal to move out. It was still dark enough that they could blend into the foliage at the base of the ridge, but after the first ten to fifteen yards of rise, they would be out in the open.

They moved through the grass without any hassles and even as they started up the gentle part of the slope, there was no response, but as more and more men emerged from the foliage a lookout spotted them and started blowing a whistle, that led to another whistle and then another.

In an instant, the top of the ridge was alive with shouting in Japanese and the flashes and pops of gunfire. When they were within twenty yards Finn called out, "Grenades! He's tagging for home!" That was his call to heave, as far as you could. Like trying to throw out a tagging runner from deep in the outfield.

The grenades flew overhead, and one, two, three explosions banged out in rapid succession. "Faster! Take the top before they can regroup!" They quickened their pace and threw another round of grenades. As they ran, his lungs burned from the acrid gunpowder smoke in the air. He looked to his left and the entire ridge was crawling with marines. It made him excited, and he topped the ridge with his rifle blasting. Pop, pop, pop,

pop, pop...ping and the magazine ejected. He was already with another one pressed to the weapon and slammed it home. He found new targets and fired again. Pop, pop. Click. Nothing. The weapon was jammed. He tried to pull the bolt, but it was open and wouldn't go forward or back. He got to his feet and saw a Japanese soldier charging him with his bayonet fixed. His face was red with fury, and he screamed as he came. Finn gave up on trying to fix it and braced for impact. As the attacker lunged into him Finn stepped aside and drove the butt of the gun across the man's jaw. He saw the man's head snap sideway in a spray of blood and teeth.

At that moment he felt a searing pain in his side and found that the bayonet struck home but didn't seem to his anything vital. He pulled free of the attacker's gun and threw his own on the ground, then drew his Ka Bar knife and his pistol.

He ran to where the fighting was heaviest and started shooting Japanese as they tried to retreat to a bunker dug into the rock. As he searched for targets, his side burned from his stab wound and then he felt a sting in his left deltoid. He had noticed it before, but didn't think much of it. *I must be hit*, he thought. But the adrenaline was coursing through his body and he just pushed forward.

He started yelling for flame throwers. Once the Japanese got inside the bunkers, they would take dozens of Americans in the fight to get them out. But a couple of blasts from the flame throwers sucked the oxygen out of the air and those that weren't burned alive were suffocated in a matter of minutes.

As he waved them up the hill, he heard a charge from his left and saw his platoon in hand-to-hand fighting. He ran forward, firing his pistol until he was out of ammo. He holstered it and picked up an entrenchment tool laying on the ground and swung it like an axe. As he jumped into the fracas, he drove the knife into a man's chest and swung the small heavy shovel, striking him on the side of the head killing him instantly. Stab, swing, stab, swing, that was the pattern as long as his adrenaline help up.

To his right he saw a soldier with a samurai sword coming at him. As the blade slashed through the air, he leaned hard to the left and brought his shovel down on the blade, then drove his knife into the man's throat. The man fell back, and Finn looked down to see that his block had driven the sword onto the side of his own leg and sliced through his pants.

He felt arms grab him and yank him back. As he struggled to turn, to the face of the rocks in front of him exploded in a sheet of flames. Men were screaming from within the bunker, and the smell of gasoline filled the air. The heat was so intense that he looked away to see that he was being dragged by Doc Clinton away from the fighting.

"You're all beat to shit McGinn," he said as he started ripping Finn's clothes to dress his wounds.

"Am I hurt bad doc?" Finn asked. Now that his battle rage was dying away, he thought about Mae and his mother and now he could feel the pain.

"Not too bad that I can see. Just hurt in a bunch of places."

When the battle was over, they made a litter and brought him back to the field station to get the bullet out of his arm and stitch his other wounds. A corpsman was handing out cigarettes, and Finn lit one up. The first drag was heavenly, but by the third puff he could feel his stomach starting to turn and snuffed it out.

When he looked up, he saw men carrying the dead down the trail on stretchers. As they grew closer, he closed his eyes and felt the tears start to sting. When he opened them again, his fears were confirmed. It was Johnny Roy, and he was shot full of holes. He thought about Joe and his parents. His mother was tiny woman, just not even five feet tall and now she'd be getting a neatly folded flag in place of her son. *She's so small and frail,* he thought. *How do they bear it?* The mere image in his mind broke him and he wept uncontrollably.

Sixteen

I t was a glorious June day, and the sun shone brightly, with only a few wisps of clouds in the sky. Allison and Melvin were making the short walk from her house to the farm. She carried Alan in her arms and rocked him occasionally, letting him drop a few inches before pretending to catch him, which led to him laughing so hard he could barely catch his breath. Jim was riding on Melvin's shoulders, holding his hands as they walked. When they reached the farm, Sean was in the yard making repairs to a hay rake he has purchased from an auction in Sparta.

"Could you use a hand?" called Melvin.

Sean picked up his head with grease smeared on his face and smiled. "Gladly."

"I'll come over in a minute."

Allison started up the steps and put Alan down on the porch then turned to help Jim off from Melvin's shoulders. He lifted the boy high in the air and brought him down to the ground.

Allison was facing him and smiled. It was a knowing smile, and he gave her the same smile back. They had a secret, and it was exciting. They stared silently for a long moment, and Allison blushed a little.

"You'd better go help Sean," she said, and Melvin grinned.

When Allison walked in smiling, Mary had a crinkled brow and her face was cast with apprehension, and Allison remembered that face all too well.

"What makes you so cheery this morning? I'm used to the angry Allison. I'm not sure what to make of a happy Allison. It makes me think something is a foot."

"It's a beautiful day, Ma, and we just had a fun walk with the boys. That's all."

Mary was still skeptical. "Well, since you're in such a fine mood. Would you peel some carrots, potatoes, and onions for me? We have a brisket Sean brined, so we're having a corned beef boiled dinner."

Allison hated peeling vegetables, especially onions. But she was determined not to let her mood be spoiled by a few onion tears. "How small do you want these onions cut?" she asked as she brought the knife down, slicing the onion in half.

Mary frowned again. "Big enough for a boiled dinner. I would have used cabbage, but there's none to be found in town."

Frances was working on rolling a pie crust and was anxious to be part of the conversation. "Thank goodness we have a farm. The rationing in town is terrible. Everything is in short supply."

It was true. Many things in town like sugar, coffee, butter, meat and canned goods were all being rationed, but the McGinns were better off than most. They had a farm that grew vegetables. Animals for meat. Chicken for eggs and milk to make butter with. Sugar and coffee were the hardest to do without, but they made up for it in recipes with honey and when they could maple syrup. Allison had a garden; Lewin had a garden at he and Cecelia's place and Sean was tending the biggest garden of them all.

Sean realized that he didn't always need as much corn as he planted for silage. They only kept a small herd now, so he dedicated part of the cornfield to beans. Great Northern Beans to be specific. They were a hearty bean and easy to grow. When they were kids, Mary used to tell them that you can grow a Great Northern bean on a rock and still get a yield.

Out in the country, there was still a lot of use of the barter system. Sean was able to trade two laying hens and a piglet for a thirty-gallon barrel of molasses. It would be enough to last them for a couple of years if they couldn't get brown sugar and if any was left when the rationing stopped, Sean thought he might try his hand at making rum.

Sean and Melvin were getting the rake back together when they heard the unmistakable rumble and popping sounds of tires on gravel. They turned to see Daisy pulling into the driveway with Lewin at her side and a carload of children in tow. They could see Lewin's face. The noise must have been making him tense, but he would never be the one to say something. He would just grit his teeth and bear it.

"That poor bastard," said Melvin with a chuckle. He was the only man in the car with Cecelia and his children. As well as Alder's wife, Daisy, and their children, Joyce and Edwin. The moment the car had rolled to a stop, the door flew open, and he nearly threw himself free of the car and gasped for air.

"A couple of those kids need changin'," he said with a laugh and got his cane steady to be able to walk. He could walk pretty well now. His biggest challenge was that his knee was so stiff from being immobilized for months and he could not run or drive himself. The cane was more of a safety blanket than anything, because he had already stumbled a few times on uneven ground at home.

"What have you got here, Sean?" Lewin asked. He looked around the farm and gave a nod of approval at how well everything looked. When he left, Pat and Alston had taken over and did a fantastic job running the farm, but somehow, Sean was doing it on his own. He was nearly seventeen, but he looked like a man. He was strong built like the McCalls and had the great smile of the McGinns. The girls had been gushing over him since he was a toddler and he gushed right back.

"I picked this rake up at a farm auction in Sparta. I gave the bank three dollars for it," he said proudly, with a broad grin. "They had lots of stuff there, but I only had three dollars and I needed a hay rake."

Lewin and Melvin stared at him silently. He was naïve and what seemed like a deal was someone else's misfortune.

"It needs a bit of work, but it was a hell of a deal." Sean grabbed the rake tines and shook them hard to show they were sturdy. "I don't think the bank made out two well, though. There were only about four men there and I just happened by when I was getting grain for the cattle and horses. "Hell of a deal, ain't she?"

Melvin studied the rake and shrugged.

"Do you know the farm it was bought from?" asked Lewin.

Sean could see that they weren't pleased and answered hesitantly. "The Elwell's farm, up near the turn to Palmyra. Why?"

Lewin sighed and Melvin gave Sean a look like a big brother looking at a child. Melvin cleared his throat. "The reason no one was there, is because the bank was taking their farm and selling everything. We don't *do* neighbors like that."

"I don't understand? I saw some of the Elwells there. I thought they wanted to sell the stuff."

Lewin bristled at that and said, "you need to pay them fair value. What do you think it's worth, Mel?"

Melvin studied it from end to end. "The hell if I know. Maybe, fifteen dollars. It's seen some work and she definitely past her prime."

"That's about where I was at too. I was thinking thirteen dollars."

Sean was completely confused now. "But I already paid for it. I got a bill of sale and everything."

Lewin leaned into his cane and stared into Sean's eyes. "We don't buy from bank auctions. That's why no one was there. The Elwells saw you buy the rake and now they likely think you were trying to take advantage of their bad luck. That's how Parker Moreland became so rich. And we're not like that. You need to give them ten more dollars to make it square."

Sean's eyes popped like boiled eggs. "I don't have ten dollars! I have about two, and I'll need that to get this rake going again."

"Give em' livestock." Suggested Melvin.

"I just traded two hens and a piglet for a barrel of molasses. Do you think they'd take a hen and a piglet? They aren't worth ten now, but by the time they're grown, they'd be worth more than that. The hen is already laying."

Lewin nodded. "I'll give you one of each, too. That will make up for the mistake and will make the apology better."

Sean shook his head and exhaled. "Jeez. I'm screwin' up plenty this week."

"Well, next week is a new week," Melvin said with a smile.

Lewin could see that something more than the rake was bothering Sean. "What's going on?"

Sean was scared. He stared at the ground, then at Melvin, then Lewin. His mouth was open, and he seemed like he was trying to form the words, but they weren't coming. He took another breath and opened his mouth again to speak...

"Boy's! Ma said come wash up for dinner!" It was Lilly bellowing across the dooryard to them.

"Can we talk after dinner?" asked Sean sheepishly.

Melvin and Lewin looked at each other and nodded.

"Sure. We'll talk in the barn after dinner," said Lewin, and they headed toward the house.

As everyone was seated, the food started being passed around. It seemed strange to Mary to see the long table so empty. She had thought about trying to store this one for big occasions and using a smaller table for her and the three children still at home. But the war would be over soon, or at least that's what she told herself, so they would need the long table for all the celebrations she had in mind.

The thought of that made her happy and as she watched everyone eating, she saw that Allison was smiling and that made her smile. Then is made her feel a bit puzzled. Allison had been bad tempered since birth, so why was she so happy now? She followed Allison's gaze, and it led to Melvin who was sitting directly across from her. He had a smile and was staring back at her.

Mary dropped her napkin and leaned down to pick it up. As she picked it up, she peered down the table to see Allison's feet entangled with Melvin's. She shot back to a sitting position and glared down the table, looking for a food item when she saw the butter at the far end.

"Allison. Pass the butter down this end. If you please."

Allison was startled a little into the present and had to get out of her seat to reach it and then passed it along.

"Thank you. If you are done eating, why don't you help me get pies cut up for dessert?" Mary said with a smile that clearly seemed forced.

"Oh, I can do that Ma," said Frances.

"No. Allison can help me. You go put some music on the radio, so we can have some entertainment with our pie."

Everyone could feel the tension and Allison wiped her mouth then headed for the kitchen. When she got there, Mary was standing with a scowl that made her displeasure quite obvious.

"What do you think you're doing?"

"What are you talking about?" Allison said a little confused.

"You and Melvin. That's why you're so happy. I know when two people are in love and I'd seen that same look in your father's eyes more than a dozen times, as you well know."

Mary could see Allison blushing. "Yes. We're sleeping together."

"Jesus, Mary and Joseph. Have you lost your damned mind, girl? You have a husband."

Now Allison flipped from embarrassed to defiant. "Yes, I do, but perhaps someone should remind him of that. He's a drunken deadbeat."

Mary shook her head. In some ways, she could empathize, but Allison was a grown woman, and she had made her own choices. "You married him and said for better or worse, forsaking all others."

"I know what I said," Allison shot back.

Mary could see the frustration boiling up in Allison's face and felt a little ashamed of being so hard on her. She had raised those two boys nearly single-handedly. She had spent more nights without her husband than with him, and she rarely complained. She just pushed on. Mary reached out and pulled Allison to her and hugged her. She kissed her on the cheek then whispered, "it's not my place to judge. But if you are going to do this, get a divorce and for God's sake, do not get pregnant."

Allison nodded and kissed Mary's cheek, then wiped the tears from her eyes. "Thank you," she croaked in a hoarse whisper.

After dinner, Sean, Melvin and Lewin stood in the barn, passing a jug of hard cider Sean had made in the fall.

"What is it you wanted to talk about?" asked Lewin.

Sean glanced around like he was about to divulge something terrible.

Lewin glared. "Oh, for Christ's sake Sean. Did you enlist?"

Sean seemed startled. "No. I promised Ma, I wouldn't enlist unless I was drafted and that won't be for another year."

Lewin relaxed. "Okay what is it?"

"Do you know the Hartley's?" Sean asked.

"Yes, of course we do. They've been our neighbors our whole life. Why?"

Sean tried to collect his thoughts. "Well, they got this cousin named Harriet Cyr, from up in the county right at the top of Maine, who came to visit last Christmas and she got herself pregnant. Now she's back."

Melvin cleared his throat, "got herself pregnant? I think the last time that happened there was a manger involved and some wise men... or something."

"Well, it was in a manger and I'm the wise man. Or dumb man probably suits better."

Lewin scowled. "You got a girl pregnant? For the love of God, Sean. How old is she?"

Sean looked at the barn floor and spoke quietly. "She had just turned fourteen."

"Oh shit," Melvin said with a shake of his head, "Mary is going to geld you."

"Only if he's lucky," added Lewin. "Where is this girl now?"

"Staying at the Hartley's farm. Her parents don't want her around showing a big belly and being unwed."

Lewin thought for a long minute. "Will they let you marry her?"

"No, her father says he'll kill me before he'd let her marry a Catholic. They're Presbyterian whatever that means."

Melvin scratched at the stubble on his face. "Doesn't sound very Christian to me."

Lewin put his hand on Sean's shoulder. "I'll talk to Ma with you, but you're on your own when she unleashes her fury."

"Great." Sean said and took another gulp of cider.

Melvin put his hand on Sean's other shoulder. "I wouldn't tell her this story drunk if I was you. You'd better ease up on the cider."

Sean tapped the cork back into the jug and sat it down on the floor. He nodded to Lewin and Melvin, then made the sign of the cross like he was about to pray.

Melvin laughed aloud. "I hope that helps."

Sean picked the jug back up and pulled the cork then took another swallow. He wiped his mouth and shrugged "Maybe another day would be better."

Seventeen

S ean sat at the table with Harriett, with Lewin and Cecelia
at flanked at each side. Harriett was a lovely girl with ash
brown hair and blue eyes. She still had a childlike look complete with a smattering of freckles across her nose and cheeks.
She couldn't have weighed more than one hundred and twenty
pounds soaking wet, and her belly was definitely showing when
she was standing.

They could hear the car pulling into the dooryard, and Sean
struggled to swallow. He heard the car door shut and the sound
of his mother's shoes on the steps. It was like something from a
horror film, and they seemed to echo loudly in his head.

When the door opened, Mary was smiling and had a small
container of strawberries. "I hope everyone like strawberry
shortcakes, because that's the dessert tonight," she said with a
smile. Then she studied Harriett. "Who's this young lady?"

Harriett blushed a little and forced a grin. "Harriett Cyr
ma'am. Pl... pleased to meet you."

Mary smiled and replied with a, "Pleased to meet you too", but her eyes were fixed on Sean. He looked like a child with a hand in the cookie jar. But she somehow knew that he hadn't been into cookies. He was in trouble. "Sean. Do you have something to say?"

Sean tried to look at his mother, but found it hard to meet her gaze, and again struggled to swallow. Then smiled at Harriett and took her hand. "Yes, Ma. Harriett... well we... I mean I."

Mary felt like she knew what was probably coming, but she was not going to let him off from the hook on something like this. "You and Harriett, what?"

"Well... we..." Sean was struggling to find the right words.

Mary was growing impatient with his stammering through whatever needed to be said. "You want to get married? Well, you are too young for that."

Sean took a deep breath. "No, that's not it. I mean yes, we do want to get married..." He paused again, searching for courage.

"I'm pregnant Mrs. McGinn." Harriett said, and slowly rose, showing her pregnant form to everyone.

Mary stood in stunned silence, trying to keep her anger and disappointment from exploding like a volcano. "How far along are you?"

Harriett stroked her rounding belly and dropped her eyes to the floor. "A little over six months ma'am."

"Her parents sent her away so as not to shame the family and her father won't let us marry and she can't keep it." Sean said.

Mary softened her tone a little. "How old are you?"

"Fourteen," replied Harriett, flushing a little with embarrassment.

"My lord. What a mess you two." Then Mary turned to Sean and glared in a way that was burning a hole in his gut. "What the hell were you thinking, Sean? She's still a child."

"Lots of people got married young, Ma." He replied with a tentative tone.

"They did. Forty years ago. How do you think that worked out for them? Fourteen-year-old girls with grown men. Or in my case a just tuned sixteen years old with a twenty-six, nearly twenty-seven-year-old man as a husband. I didn't know what I was doing and now I'm a widow with eleven children."

"We're only three years apart, Ma," he lightly protested.

"I realize that, son, but there is a big step in those three years, when you're fourteen years old, and why did you spill your seed inside her? Are you simple, son?"

Sean and Harriett both squirmed and blushed. "It felt good," muttered Sean.

Mary bit her lip in exasperation. "Good God. I don't even know what to say to that." Then she realized the other people that were present and turned to Lewin and Cecelia. "What have you two got to do with this? Are you looking to adopt the baby?"

Cecelia shook her head no. "If it came down to it, we would, but we have another idea we'd like to explore first."

"What is that?" Mary asked.

Lewin patted Harriett on the shoulder. "There are some people we know that might help out, but I'd like to talk with them first before we go any further."

"I hope you do find someone. I'm too old to raise any babies, so I hope they are good people."

Lewin smiled. "They are. They are the very best."

Emma was sitting the front window of the store sewing pearls into a wedding dress when the bell over the door rang. It was Lewin and Cecelia and Emma burst into a smile. "Oh Lew, Celia, it's so nice to see you." She jumped up and gave them each a huge hug.

"It's always nice to see you, Emma. That dress is a beauty," Cecelia said, admiring the pearl work.

Emma smiled. "Oh thanks. I love making wedding dresses. Each one is so unique." Then she saw two people in the back seat of their car. "Who's with you?" She squinted to see. "Is that Sean?"

Lewin nodded. "Yes. He wants to talk to you and Bill, but he needs to talk to you together."

Emma squinted to see who else was in the car and crinkled her brow like something was fishy. "He's helping unload meat out back, but I can get him."

"That would be great," said Cecelia and Emma started to the back. "And Emma." She stopped and turned back to Cecelia and Lewin. Cecelia smiled. "This is a good thing."

Emma went into the back room and came back with Bill in tow. While Emma was in the back, Lewin had motioned for Sean and Harriett to come inside.

Bill smiled at seeing his in-laws. "Lew. What's going on?" and as he asked, the bell over the door rang and Sean and Harriett stepped inside. The dress that Harriett wore was oversized and didn't reveal her belly to the public.

"I'll let Sean tell you," Lewin said and motioned for Sean to speak.

Sean stood literally with his hat in his hand as he rang the life out of his fedora. "Bill, Emma. I would like to ask a favor."

Bill glanced at Harriett and sighed. "We really aren't looking for any help right now, Sean."

"It's bigger than that," Sean said sheepishly.

Then Emma had made enough maternity dresses to realize what was actually happening. "My God. She's pregnant."

Harriett blushed and her eyes started to fill with tears. Then turned her face to hide that she was about to cry.

"She is. With my baby. But her father won't let her keep it or us get married on account of her age and all. We don't want it to go to an orphanage."

Bill stood with his mouth open and seemed as if he could be knocked over with a feather. He hadn't expected that. He and Emma had tried as much as any couple, but in six years, she had never even been pregnant once. Not even a miscarriage. He knew how badly she wanted a child and he wanted to give it to her. "Can we talk this over and get back to you?" he asked.

Emma was horrified at the thought of not saying yes, but she trusted Bill.

"Of course," Sean said, and they proceeded to tell Bill and Emma about Harriett's life in the county.

After they left, Bill sat with Emma. "You know that my sole purpose in life is to bring you as much joy as you have brought me. Right?"

Emma reached out and squeezed his hand. "I know that. You always treat me like a queen. But why are you saying that? Do you not want to do it? I don't want you to say yes just to make me happy."

He nodded. "So, you want this? To adopt that baby? Do you not want to keep trying on or own?"

"I want us to have our baby. But I want this baby to have a happy, loving home. Our home."

Bill smiled and leaned in to kiss her cheek. He stared into her eyes, and she begged him with her gaze back at him. He thought that she might burst with waiting to hear his answer. "Me too. I'll have John Maxwell draw up papers in the morning. She can stay with us or with my mother whichever you think is best."

Emma squealed with excitement and threw her arms around him, kissing his face over and over. "Thank you, Bill. I love you so much."

He smiled and held her. "And I love you. I can't wait to tell my mother. She'll be over the moon."

The next day, they told Sean of their decision and Mary couldn't think of a better couple than her own daughter and son-in-law. It was like a weight had been lifted from her. She had legitimately feared that she would somehow be raising yet another baby.

John Maxwell drew up the contract and mailed a copy to the Cyr's in Frenchville and had Sean sign a copy here. Bill loved his family and in-laws, but he didn't want any chance of a custody dispute no matter how unlikely.

Harriett moved into the house at the Moreland Farm, in Bill's old room, and Miss Rose was so excited that people might have thought that she was the one about to give birth.

Eighteen

July 4th, 1943

Allison loved the fourth of July festivities in Monroe. Outside of the fair, it was her favorite time in the summer. The town went all out with parades and public barbecues. Music all day and into the evening and then, of course, the fireworks. She loved to bring a blanket and lay on her back just watching the sky as rockets burst. She was trying to teach the boys to enjoy it as well, but neither was ever able to stay awake late enough to see it. She was envious of how they could sleep through everything. Even the sounds of rockets screaming through the air and explosions that shook the sky.

As she and Melvin walked through town, she pushed Alan in a carriage and Jim rode on Melvin's shoulders. They stopped and talked to people they knew, and everyone loved to see Jim. He was adorable and old ladies loved to pinch his cheeks and poke his dimples. Beyond being a cute child, he was an incessant talker. He never stopped talking and Mary said that it must be the name because her Jim was the same way.

As they watched the parade, Jim went wild at the sight of the firetrucks and bounced wildly up and down on Melvin's shoulders, clapping.

"I see he's doing much better now," came a voice from beside him. It was Tom Diamond, and he had a big smile and tugged at Jim's foot.

Melvin seemed puzzled by that statement. "He's doing fine. It's getting him to sit still that's the challenge."

Now it was Tom's turn to be puzzled. "I thought he had polio. Or at least that is what I was told."

Allison turned a little annoyed. "No, it was my brother's son Alvin, that died from polio. But that was years ago."

Tom frowned. "So, this child hasn't been sick?"

"God no. He's healthy as a mule and just as stubborn," Melvin said with a chuckle.

Allison could see Tom's face turning red with anger. "Why would you think he was sick?"

Tom sighed and spat on the ground. "Because about a month ago, your husband saw me coming out of a store and laid a tale on me about his son having polio and needing to be rushed to the children's hospital in Watertown."

Allison's jaw dropped. "I hate him", she said as her eyes filled with tears.

Melvin picked Jim from his shoulders and put him on the ground. "Tom. I am sorry. Please know that we had nothing to do with this. That little son of a bitch hasn't even told anyone that he was home. Is he still in the Navy?"

Tom shook his head. "I don't know. He wasn't wearing sailor clothes. I thought about talking to you first, but he said you two were in Watertown with the boy."

Melvin was embarrassed to even be his brother. "How much did he get Tom? I'll pay you back myself."

Allison sniffled. "We both will."

Tom chuckled. "Don't worry about it. It was one-hundred dollars."

Allison gasped, and Melvin bit his lip and turned his head from side to side, then reached into his pocket for his wallet. "Don't worry about one-hundred dollars? That's a month's pay for me."

Tom stopped him. "Put that away. I had just come from the racetrack and those were only part of my winnings. So, I'm fine. But I take it you two wouldn't be offended if I were to beat the tar out of him, if I ever see him again?"

Melvin shook head. He held out his hand to shake with Tom. "Whoever gets to him first, let the other one know, so that they can have a turn. Sound fair?"

"Sounds fair to me, and truly don't worry about it, Mel. I've known you a long time and your brother would never be a reflection of you. In fact, I feel kind of sorry for you."

Allison wiped the tears from her eyes. "Thank you, Mr. Diamond. It means a lot to me that you would have done that for my son."

145

"You're welcome, dear," he said and patted her on the shoulder. "That little bastard is a real convincing liar. But I won't be fooled again."

As Tom walked away, Allison stared at Melvin. "Why does he do these things? Why is he so rotten? He's bad right to his core."

Melvin shrugged. "I don't know. He was like this as a child and I thought he might outgrow it, but I think that if anything, he's gotten worse."

"How can you two be so different?" she asked.

"Alcohol. It's the only logical thing."

A few days later, Melvin was in town buying parts for his saw Whitson's Equipment when he ran into Bob Mercier. Bob was a great war veteran, local gossip monger and professional loiterer. He held court for hours in whatever store would let him hang about. Melvin sometimes wondered if he ever drove off business with all of his yapping.

"Saw your brother last week." Bob leaned against the counter with his belly hanging out through his suspenders. He had a smirk that made Melvin inclined to slap his face, but he restrained himself.

"Oh yeah. Was he running for his life?" Melvin quipped back.

"Nope. He was at the Elm Hotel in Watertown. Drunk as a lord and shooting his mouth off."

"That sounds like him."

"People say he had spent so much time in the brig onboard ship that the captain convinced the Navy to give him the choice of getting out on a Bad Conduct discharge."

"Once again, that sounds like him." He went about his business looking for parts, trying to cut the conversation short without being too rude.

"They deprived him of veteran benefits, but he was given the choice of that or spend the next ten years in Leavenworth doing hard labor, and that would have deprived him of his freedom. So, I guess he chose to get out."

Melvin shrugged. "Probably would have been better if he went to prison. He'd be less apt to get into trouble that way."

"He said some things about you as well."

Melvin picked through the nuts and bolts looking for some spares to keep around the barn. "Really? And what was that?"

"Says you're sleeping with his wife, and that you stole his family."

Melvin noticed Bob grinning. "Well, he wouldn't know, since he's the one who abandoned them."

"Well, people around town wonder what's going on out there. I mean she's married... and you're his brother. That don't seem right to folk around here. At least that's what I'm hearin'."

Melvin put his parts down and moved close to Bob. He got close enough to whisper so that no one else could hear. "The lady's beauty parlor is just down the street. Why don't you go gossip there? You'll be at home with the rest of the old biddies."

Bob pulled back and scowled.

Melvin chuckled. "Your tits are big enough. You'll fit right in with the saggy old ladies down there."

Bob pulled back and slapped his hand down on the counter. "Why the hell would you say something like that? I never done you wrong."

"True enough. But if I'm being completely honest. I just don't care for you."

Bob stood with his mouth gaped open, looking for something to say.

"You're a Yankees fan Bob. Nobody likes you. Everyone knows that Yankee fans are assholes."

Bob slapped the counter again, and his face was becoming flushed. "You...you...son of a bitch!" He grabbed his cap from the counter and stormed off out the door.

Barney Whitson watched him go and turned to Melvin with a smile. "Thank you! He is the most talkin'est, know-it-all SOB I've ever known. People see him in here and they walk by. I know they do."

"He does love the sound of his own voice. That's for damn sure."

Barney pulled the parts into a pile in front of him. "That going to do it for you, Mel?"

Melvin nodded. "Yeah, that should get me by for now." He was still watching the door to see if Mercier was coming back to have another go at him. But he never did.

"Who cares what people think," Barney said interrupting Melvin' thoughts.

"How's that?" Melvin asked.

"You and your brother's wife. Who cares what people think? There's already a couple of women in town pregnant and their husbands have been gone for over a year. Nobody has room to cast stones."

Melvin nodded. "I don't care because nothing is going on. She helped me recover from surgery and I help her at the farm. That's it. Nobody's business."

"That's what I've been saying," Barney said with a smile.

Melvin took his bag of parts and left. As he walked down the street, he had a feeling that people were looking and staring, whispering as he passed. He started to feel anxious and found it hard to fill his lungs. He picked up his pace and walked to the truck without making eye contact. He hopped in and closed the door, trying to catch his breath. When he glanced around, there were people on the street, everywhere.

But there was something strange. No one was looking at him. No one was whispering. People were going about their business like any other day. Then he thought about the absurdity of it all. He knew some people in town, but most people wouldn't know who the hell he was. He looked up and down the street and didn't recognize anyone except Bob Mercier who was headed to the barbershop.

Melvin laughed and thought to himself. *Maybe. Just maybe, people don't care about us half as much as we think they do. I guess they have their own shit to worry about.*

Nineteen

August 2, 1943

Melvin stood in the woodyard at Orwell manufacturing while Tom Diamond unloaded his bolt wood. He was impressed by the scale of the operation. The factory had once been a simple lumber mill, and everything was done with horses. But now that Virgil Orwell owned it, it was a large-scale modern operation. The din of saw and lathes at work was deafening and even outside he had to shout to be heard.

"Quite an operation!" he yelled to Tom.

"Yeah, Orwell is a smart man. He owns everything war related in town!" replied Tom.

Orwell was a shrewd businessman and an even shrewder opportunist. He had converted his shoe factory to a boot factory, and they were churning out boots for the military by the thousands every month.

Soon after the attack on Pearl Harbor, he found himself in New Haven, Connecticut on business and had a chance meeting with a local businessman who had secured a contract to make M-1 carbine rifles. Being a businessman, Orwell turned two cigars and four bourbons into an agreement to supply gunstocks for the rifles. When he returned to Maine, he bought the Anderson sawmill across the river from Monroe and quickly turned it into a gunstock factory. Anderson and his son retired wealthy men and Orwell became even wealthier.

The place was bustling with activity and two boys jumped up on the back of the truck and stood atop the massive pile of timber. One tugged at the unloading cables while the other guided a massive hook into the loops at the cable ends. They jumped clear of the back section, waving their arms, and the small crane that unloaded the trucks roared into action. As the tension grew on the cable, a whole section of wood began to rise from the truck bed. The massive weight was clenched tightly together by the cables. The load rocked gently back and forth as the crane arm made its ponderous swing to the woodpile, then it dropped suddenly, and Melvin's *bolt wood* was added to the heap. They repeated the process three more times until the truck was empty.

When it was done, Diamond collected payment from the yard clerk and gave Melvin his share.

"Not a bad payday, ha Mel?"

Melvin fanned through the bills and smiled. It was far more than they had ever gotten for softwood at the paper mill. "Not bad at all."

"Can I interest you in a cold beer at the Midtown?" Tom asked.

"No. I don't drink. Never have."

Tom smiled. "I know, but I figured I'd offer, anyway."

"I've got to get headed back and start working on my next load."

Melvin jumped in the truck and started back to the house. *Allison will be impressed that the paycheck actually made it home*, he thought.

He drove through town and headed toward the country club. It was hot and sticky with air so thick you could almost drink it. The breeze of driving felt good on his face. As he drove past the golf course, he felt a little sad because it looked so deserted. The country club had always been busy, but with so many men away at war, it seemed a shadow of its former self.

He was driving down Howell Hill Road and saw a hitchhiker in the distance. He was only going another couple of miles, so he didn't plan on stopping. But as he got closer, the hiker seemed familiar and when he was upon him, he stomped on the brakes, leaving a blinding cloud of dust that enveloped the truck and the hiker.

Melvin shut off the truck and jumped out. He practically ran around the front and grabbed the hiker by the collar. "You! What the hell are you doing here you low-life son-of-a-whore?!"

The hiker pushed Melvin off and brushed the dust from his clothes. "That's no way to talk about our mother," said Calvin.

Melvin could feel the blood boil in his veins and used all his self-restraint to keep from beating his brother to death right here. "What do you want?"

"How about a lift home, to see my wife and sons?" Calvin said with a smirk.

"Which son would that be, the one who doesn't know you or the one with Polio?"

Calvin's smile disappeared. "How'd you hear about that?"

"Tom Diamond and I are partners on a woods operation."

Calvin paused for a moment. "Well, I saw he won some money at the racetrack. I didn't have any luck, but he had a fist full of bills, so I..."

"Lied? Cheated? Stole? What kind of man are you?"

"Lying? Aren't you laying with my wife every night? That's what people in town are saying."

Melvin half expected that. Especially after people had seen them together on the 4th of July. "You abandoned her and your children. You're not welcome there anymore. So, you'd best be heading back to town," he said with a jerk of his thumb.

"It's my house! You self-righteous asshole!"

Melvin snapped off a jab that caught Calvin square in the mouth. He staggered back and wiped the blood from his lip. His face turned to a mask of rage, and he charged at Melvin, who stepped to his left and buried his fist in Calvin's gut knocking the wind from him. Calvin was always so predictable. Nearly every fight they had ever led to Calvin charging him, Melvin stepping aside and punching him in the gut. *Damn, he's a slow learner*, thought Melvin.

Calvin dropped to his knees, and after a long moment gasped for air. "You cocksucker." He gasped again. "I'll fuckin' kill you."

Melvin laughed at him. "You'll need to be sober first. Not much risk of that."

Calvin gasped again and caught his breath. "They're *my* family Melvin."

Melvin shook his head in disgust. "You never acted like they were, and now she doesn't want you. You only want to go there because you have nowhere else to go."

"She's, my wife!"

Melvin stood looming over Calvin. A man with less restraint might have beaten him senseless, right there and left him in the ditch, but Melvin no longer cared for him enough to do that. "Let me know where you're staying so I can have the sheriff serve you with divorce papers."

"Fuck you and fuck her. I'm not divorcing that little tramp and I'm taking my house back!"

Melvin grabbed him by the hair and dragged him to the truck, then pounded his head off from the bumper twice and pushed him to the ground. "Get out of town. Now. When I get to the store, I'm going to use their telephone to call Tom Diamond and tell him where you are. I wouldn't want to be on the road if I was you."

Calvin staggered to his feet with blood running down the side of his head. "You're not my brother. You're a Judas."

Melvin laughed out loud. "You? Referencing the bible? That's the funniest damned thing I've heard in a long time. Stay away from the farms. The McGinns don't want you around either."

Calvin chuckled in feigned bravado. "All the men are away at war. The McGinns don't scare me."

Melvin shrugged. "Aaron McCall isn't at war, and I think he'd love to have a go with you. Daniel McCall isn't at war, and I know he'd like to snap you over his knee."

"I've got no money Melvin. I have no place to go."

Melvin shook his head. "I'm not giving you a thing except advice. Get out of town. Jump a train. Become a hobo. I don't care, just don't come back. Ever."

Calvin looked defeated. His lip and head were bleeding, and he was covered in dirt. "Give me an hour before you call Diamond so I can get away?"

"You have until I get to the store. Chances are he's not home. He was headed to the Midtown when I left him, so that might buy you some time."

Calvin spat blood on the ground. "I hate you. You're not my brother."

"You said that already and that's fine with me. I never considered you to be mine." Melvin regretted it as soon as the words left his lips. But there was no taking it back.

Calvin looked like he had been gut punched again. He had made his statement in anger, but the way Melvin said it was like he meant it.

Then Melvin climbed back into the truck and drove away without another word. He watched Calvin in the mirror as he drove away. Calvin just stood there staring at the truck like Melvin might have a change of heart and come back. Eventually, he gave up and started walking back toward town.

When he stopped at the store, he went inside and picked up the phone, but didn't activate the receiver for the operator. He stood thinking.

Emma watched him from where she was sewing and paused. "Melvin. Is everything alright?"

He hung up the earpiece. "Yeah. Can I get a carton of camels and a fifth of bourbon?"

Emma was shocked and stared in amazement.

"Can I get those? I have cash."

She snapped back to reality and said, "yes, of course."

She put the bourbon and cigarettes in a bag, took his money and gave him his change. She was still too shocked to speak.

Melvin smiled. "Thanks Em. See you at Sunday dinner." Then he left the store and drove away.

He drove for a way past where he and Calvin had just fought. He could see him far in the distance. At the sight of the approaching vehicle, Calvin jumped into the woods. Melvin slowed down in the area where Calvin had disappeared and saw him trying to hide in the bushes. Then stopped.

"Come here!" Melvin yelled.

"No! I don't want to see you!"

"I have something for you!"

Calvin peeked out. "I don't want it!"

Melvin parked the truck and stepped out. Calvin retreated a little further into the woods.

"You're trying to stall until Diamond gets here!"

Melvin placed the bag on the ground and pulled a couple of bills and some change from his pocket and dropped them into the bag so that Calvin could see. Then he opened the door to the truck to get back in and stopped. He turned to Calvin. "Don't ever come back here again. I don't want to have to give you to Tom. But I will next time. I swear it."

He climbed into the truck and pulled ahead, backed up, and turned the truck back toward home. He watched him again in the mirror and Calvin looked in the bag. He pulled out the bottle and took the money, stuffing it in his pocket. He looked at the truck driving away and took a swig from the bottle, then held the bottle and carton up high in the air.

Melvin heard him yell something, but he couldn't make out whether it was "Thank you" or "Fuck you." But he really didn't care either way.

He wasn't sure why he didn't call Tom. Or why he bought the vices he despised so much in his brother? Maybe it was guilt for sleeping with his wife and taking his family. Maybe it was just the best way to say goodbye to his brother.

When he got home, he relayed the story to Allison. At first, she was angry that he would try to show up now after all this time, and even angrier that Melvin would give him booze and money. But then, somewhere in her heart, she felt some pity for him. She thought about how charming and good looking he was when he swept her off her feet. But that image was replaced by the memory of her sweeping her off her feet again and slamming her to the floor.

Maybe it was guilt over her relationship with Melvin? Or maybe she felt like the boys should know their father?

She had never been happier than now, and the boys adored Melvin. They never went hungry, and she and Melvin were a great team and they truly loved each other. When she thought back about Calvin, she wondered if he loved anyone or anything as much as himself.

Twenty

M ary stood at the table making biscuit dough and listening to the radio. The dining room was empty, and the absurdly large table now seemed like some kind of sick joke to mock her. She loved Sunday dinners with her children and grandchildren, but now people didn't come around as much.

After Lewin returned, he and Cecelia made it to a couple of dinners, but he was still having great difficulty getting around. Allison and Melvin came frequently, but it didn't feel special to her because she saw them nearly every day. It was the same with Daisy. They worked together, and she loved Daisy, but when you see someone all day every day you run out of interesting topics of conversation. Mae was still working every other weekend and was still on the night shift, so she was usually looking to get some sleep. At least she could rely on Bill and Emma. They were the most consistent. They spent so many hours at the store, that they rarely had the energy to fix a proper meal, so Sunday dinner was a treat.

Mary was happy that they were coming today because her grandchild would be coming any day now. Harriett had moved into the main house at the Moreland farm and was being pampered by Bill's mother Rose to the point of smothering the poor girl. Sean had gotten himself into a real mess and thankfully his sister was there to bail him out.

The dough felt good between her fingers and she both loved and despised listening to the radio. She loved the music from the Philco, but every news break left her with her heart in her throat. More than once, Frances had chided her for over-kneading the dough. Her mind was off somewhere, on a Pacific Island, or under the ocean, or in England. Her sons- and son-in-law were scattered across the globe. She lived for any news about what might be happening, and yet dreaded hearing anything about the war. She just wanted her sons back home. Finn and Patrick had both been wounded, but not enough to come home yet. Or perhaps they stayed on their own accord.

John Roy was dead, and his family wouldn't be able to retrieve his body until after the war was over. The thought of her boys buried on the other side of the world made her sick, so she tried to turn her mind to something else.

Mercifully, her thoughts were interrupted by the sound of Lillian crashing through the door with a huge basket full of vegetables from the garden. The basked was filled to overflowing.

Mary smiled. "Wonderful. Start peeling potatoes and carrots."

Lillian dropped the basket with a groan. "God that was heavy." She bent over to catch her breath. "How many are eating?"

Mary thought for a moment. "Make enough for ten. Whatever is left we'll give to one of your sisters."

Lillian pulled a dozen potatoes from the basket along with a couple pounds carrots. "What are we having with it, Ma?"

"Irish stew. We have some canned mutton in the pantry."

Lillian frowned and made a face. "It smells funny, Ma. And tastes funny too."

"Mutton has a distinct smell to be sure. But there are plenty of people eating no meat in town, so if you'd prefer you can go to town and eat with them."

Lillian was thinking about what to say next, but her senses came to bear, and she grinned without speaking.

"That's what I thought. Now start peeling. Do you have any onions in there?"

"Yes, a few yellow ones." Lillian said and started to wash the vegetables.

"Good. Throw the biggest one in. If we have a turnip, throw that in too. There is only one jar of mutton."

Lillian cut all the vegetables into large sized cubes. Not so large as to make them hard to chew, and not so small that they'd become mush after a long simmer.

Mary went back to her biscuit making. It was an odd day. It was the first time in twenty-five years that she hadn't used Clabber Girl baking powder. With the war effort having to feed so many men, it was nearly impossible to get baking powder now. Instead, she was using Bakewell Cream. It was a baking powder of sorts, and many people liked it. Most probably liked it because it was made in Maine, so in their minds, it had to be a quality product.

"I hope those rise," Lilian said, looking at Frances and pointing at the pan of biscuits in front of Mary.

"Well, if they don't it's because she squeezed them to death," Frances said with a smile.

"Hush girls. They'll rise. I'll stake my apron on it." They both were skeptical. "If they don't rise, I'll do the dishes myself tonight. But when they do, you two do them and I'll put my feet up and watch."

The girls both nodded, "agreed," they said in unison.

Alder sat on a bench across from Dooley's Public House. It was his favorite place in England. Unfortunately, it was the favorite place of hundreds of soldiers, so getting a drink was always a hassle. The men would crowd in, to the point that no one could really move or hear each other. The whole experience was a combination of noise, stale beer smell, and body odor. Particularly in the summer. It wasn't really hot like at home, but having that many men in one spot made the air unmerciful.

His favorite part of being in England was that Alston was there, and they saw each other every week or so. Joe Roy was somewhere in England as well, but they hadn't seen him yet, and today was the day. It was the first time they would all be together since they rode to the train station on their way to their boot camps.

Alder wasn't sure how it would be to see Joe now that his brother John was dead. Growing up, Alder had never been particularly religious, but he had prayed more since leaving for war than the whole rest of his life combined. So far, everyone was safe, and Lewin was already home. They weren't without their wounds, but at least they were alive.

"Hey old man!" he heard a familiar voice call out from down the street. It was Alston. He was beaming from ear to ear and walked with long strides toward him.

"Hey young man," he replied, and embraced his brother. "You're looking well."

Alston smiled. "Thanks. Have you heard from home lately?"

"I got a letter from Daisy two weeks ago saying Sean *knocked up* some girl from the county and she's due any day now. May have had it by now. Nothing since then. You?"

Alston nodded. "Yeah. I heard about that in my last letter. Ma said that Emma and Bill are going to adopt the baby."

"Thank God for that," said Alder. "Sean can barely tend animals; he'd be dangerous with a child."

Alston reached into his back pocket and pulled out a thick envelope. Alder could see by the handwriting that it was from their mother.

Alder's eyes seemed to twinkle with excitement. "What's it say?"

Alston flipped the envelope over to reveal that it had not been opened. "We can find out together," he said, grinning.

They were like two schoolgirls with a secret, and both nearly giggled with excitement. Alston ripped the seam of the envelope carefully to keep it more or less intact. When he finally opened the letter, he realized that it was several letters from his mother and his sisters. Included were a number of photographs. It seems that Frances had purchased a Kodak Brownie camera and was making everyone crazy with her photography. There were pictures Sean working the farm, their mother making biscuits, Allison and the boys, Ruth at the diner, Daisy and Mae leaning against a car and Lillian with her prized chicken ready for the Monroe Fair.

Alder studied the photos and touched the picture of Daisy. He missed her terribly. "They appear happy. I just hope Daisy isn't teaching Mae to drive," he said with a laugh.

"Well, didn't you teach Daisy to drive?" asked Alston.

Alder frowned. "Yes. What's your point?"

"Seems to me that the student is only as good as the teacher."

Alder punched him hard, but playfully in the arm. "You little bastard. You're supposed to be on my side."

Alston rubbed his arm. "I am you stooge."

They heard a voice calling out. "Break it up you two!" and they turned to see Joe Roy walking toward them. He was so muscular that he might have been carved from granite. His uniform was impeccable, and he wore a hat with a paratrooper patch.

The three men shook hands and embraced. Alder smiled. "It's really good to see you, Joe."

Joe nodded. "Same. Good to see pieces of home."

Alston met his gaze with sad eyes. "I was sorry to hear about Johnny. He was a hell of a guy. I remember cutting ice with you guys. He was stronger than most of the men and he was only fifteen."

"Thanks. My sister Theresa said my folks took it real hard, and the government isn't sending any bodies home until the war is over."

Alder shook his head. "Damn. I had heard that, but it's hard to believe. So many men killed and buried all over the globe. Doesn't seem right."

Joe sighed. "They can't spare the ships for that. They need every ship for the war effort."

"Still don't seem right. Their families will want them in their family plots," added Alston.

"Ruth said that Finn got shot up on the same hill. But he's staying in?"

Alder shrugged. "I guess the bullet was a ricochet, so it was near the surface and the other wounds just needed stitches."

Joe shook his head. "He is one tough SOB. That's for sure." They all nodded. "So was John, but it was his time, I guess." There was a long pause. "Any news from home?"

Alston's mood changed to a much more positive aspect. He pulled the envelope from his trouser pocket and flipped through the photographs. He plucked the picture of Ruth at the diner. She was standing behind the counter with a pot of coffee in one hand and a slice of pie on a small plate in the other. "Here's something for you," he said and handed the picture to Joe.

Joe saw the picture and his face lit up. "She's so beautiful," he croaked in a voice that sounded like it was about to break. He sniffled and wiped at his eyes for a moment. "I miss her awfully bad."

That made Alder think about Daisy. He patted Joe on the shoulder. "It's not easy. That's for damn sure."

Alston gave them a moment for quiet reflection, then tried to lighten the mood. "I have a surprise for you two."

"I could use a surprise," said Joe. "What is it?"

Alston reached into his pocket and pulled out a flask, and shook it back and forth. "It's Irish."

Alder sniffed at the flask somewhat suspect. "Jesus, Alston, it's not the Poteen, is it?"

Alston laughed. "No, it's Jameson's. The best whiskey."

Joe held out a hand. "Don't be stingy now," and Alston handed over the flask.

Joe opened the top and sniffed. "This is nice. You boys mind if I say a little something in the way of a toast?"

"Of course," muttered Alder.

Joe took a deep breath. "To my brother John. I'll miss you more than you'll know. May the lord keep you close and bring the rest of us home to our loved ones." He took a big swig and held it in his mouth for a moment before swallowing. Then nodded in approval.

Alder smiled at his brother- and brother-in-law. "Amen to that."

Twenty–One

November 1943

It was the Monday before Thanksgiving. Sean sat on a stump, trying not to breathe too hard. The fog from his breath made it hard to see, so he tried to breathe down to keep his cloud to a minimum. He loved this spot and had gotten deer from here three years in a row. It had a perfect line of sight to a line of apple trees at the lower end of the field. They tried to keep as many apples as they could, but he made sure to leave a decent number of drops around for the deer herd.

At the end of the harvest, he always had some extra corn around, so he made sure to leave that lying under the trees as well.

He could feel the morning chill creeping through his pants as he sat on the cold stump and shifted carefully to let his backside warm up a little. As he sat, he started to think about Harriett and the baby they had given to Emma and Bill. It made him feel bad, but somehow it was the only plan that made sense. He would have married her, but her father would have none of that. Their passion was real. When he saw her for the first time, he just thought she was beautiful. She was only fourteen, but she was a woman to him. When he finally got a chance to show her the barn, he looked into her eyes, and she wouldn't stop staring at him. When he kissed her, he felt a swelling in his pants and when he pulled her close, she felt it, too. She touched it and he thought he might lose his mind and then he just acted. They dropped their small clothes, and he was inside her, kissing her, and then it was done. Mere seconds of ecstasy.

She came up to the farm every day for a week, and they re-played the same scene over and over. They would get alone and each time it lasted a little longer until finally they understood what all the fuss was about. He was sad to see her go and was looking forward to her return in the summer. But she went back to the county and a month later realized that she was pregnant.

He imagined he loved her. Or at least what he thought love was. She made him happy, and she seemed to be happy with him. Why wouldn't her father let her marry him? People married young all the time. McGinns are hard workers and he figured he'd be a pretty good husband. It didn't seem fair.

When he snapped back from his contemplations. He scanned the field and saw two deer eating apples and corn. His day-dreaming nearly cost him many meals.

Sean contemplated the two deer. One large buck and one spike horn. The buck was right next to the tree and the spike horn was right behind him. Sean pulled the lever-action Winchester to his shoulder very slowly and aimed through the sights. A clear shot at the buck, which was standing perpendicular to him, showing his whole right side. Then he swung the barrel to the spike horn and saw his chest facing him.

As he was about to swing back to the buck, a thought crossed his mind. If I'm quick, I can have them both. He had practiced with the 30-30 as much as he could. Training to shoot multiple targets in succession in case he was ever called to war. Practice was everything. Sometimes it was the difference between meat and potatoes or just potatoes for the winter, so he wanted to be sure about his weapon.

He lined the spike horn up in his sights and barely touched the trigger. His brothers had taught him that pulling the trigger with your whole finger made the shot less accurate. He relaxed and took a deep breath and, on the exhale, he squeezed the trigger and immediately racked the lever and took aim at the buck. The big male jumped to attention and as it was about to spring, when he squeezed the trigger again. The buck jumped forward and stumbled onto its face. When it tried to rise again, it dropped. Sean glanced back to the spike horn, who was bounding away, and he racked the lever again and squeezed off a third shot. The spike horn disappeared into the woods and Sean ran toward the apple trees.

When he neared the trees, he could see that the buck was dead, so he ran to where he had last seen the spike horn. There was a clear blood trail and he rushed into the woods. Tracking was easy with all the broken branches and bloody leaves making a path into thicker woods. He could hear the animal wheezing and slowed his approach. It was lying on the ground, gasping for air. It was shot it in the chest and probably had collapsed a lung. The deer stared at Sean with its great black eye. It was filled with terror.

Sean pulled his hunting knife from his sheath and moved up to the wounded animal. He had contemplated shooting it again, but what if it lingered on? He just wanted it dead. As he planned the final blow, he felt melancholy all of a sudden and couldn't look at the deer. "God forgive me," he whispered and dropped to his knees, grasped one of the horns and buried the knife to the hilt up under the base of the skull then twisted. In an instant, the deer stopped struggling and Sean felt a grumble in his stomach. Sean pictured the baby that he and Harriett had conceived, then, a moment later, his breakfast came spewing from his mouth and he leaned forward and retched all over the ground.

Sean had never felt this before, but somehow the thought of taking a life bothered him. He had killed many animals and always been pleased with himself, but not today and not this young buck. Maybe that is what it meant to be a father. That helpless baby. As helpless as a wounded young deer lying on the frost covered leaves of the Maine woods. An overwhelming sense of guilt washed over him.

On Thursday it was Thanksgiving. Sean did the front quarter of the young buck the way that Alston had taught him with it wrapped in bacon, at a low heat. Everyone raved about the venison, how it melted in their mouths, but he couldn't bring himself to even try a bite. When he looked at the carved meat and his heart sunk. *I should have just taken one,* he thought.

He watched Emma holding the fat little infant Daniel that he and Harriett had made, and she was genuinely happy. So happy that he thought she could not be happier if she lived to be one-hundred years old. In his heart, he knew that they had done the right thing, but he thought about Harriett and what she might be doing right now.

Sean missed her and he felt ashamed that he had made her pregnant. She was so strong for a girl of fourteen. The day she left to return to the county he met her at the train station. When she saw him, her face was something between happy and melancholy. Her bright eyes glistened as she fought back tears. She took a deep breath and stood up straight. A forced smile crept across her face.

"I'm glad you came," she said and reached out to touch his hand.

Sean stepped forward and was about to hug her, when she placed a hand on his chest and gently held him off. "What's wrong?"

"I can't. If I let you hold me, I might never stop crying." She squeezed his hand hard. "Please watch over our son. Be a good uncle."

Sean felt cold wet streaks on his face and realized he was crying. He sniffed and wiped his face in a quick motion in the hope that no one would notice. "Not manly to cry."

"That's foolish. Everyone was made to cry. That's why God made tears." She released her grip and slid her hand away with the lightest touch. "I'll miss you, Sean McGinn."

"Me too," he said, and she grinned and nodded. She boarded the train and sat in a window seat. As the train moved away, he watched and when she finally looked, he stood tall and waved, trying to keep a smile on his face. She nodded again and that was the last time he would ever see her.

Finn sat with Freddie Dumond in their fox hole divvying up what food they had. They had meat and beans and meat and potatoes, a chocolate bar, some dried bread that was something akin to a thick cracker but even less desirable than a saltine. Freddie had some fudge and Finn had a pack of Camel cigarettes. It was all that could be expected from a C Ration. A day's food in cans. Early in a campaign, they were disgusting and most of the men griped. By their second month on Guadalcanal, men might have fought each other to the death for one of those damned biscuits.

This was their Thanksgiving dinner. No turkey, no pie, not even a slice of fresh bread. They sat telling stories about family traditions. The Dumond's always hunted in the morning on Thanksgiving. Freddie had shot his first deer on a Thanksgiving. It had always thrilled him to hunt deer, but now he felt differently. He had killed at least ten men, that he knew of. He had no idea how many he had killed with grenades, but now the thought of shooting a deer seemed pointless. *I could buy meat or go without*, he thought.

Finn had a different perspective about hunting. With fourteen people to feed his father's philosophy was always, *take what you need and eat what you take*. Finn never developed a love of hunting, but there was a practicality about it. They ate every morsel and used every piece of the deer possible. Over the years, Mary had become very good at making deerskin mittens and moccasins.

When they finished eating, they read letters from home to each other. When Finn came to the parts about how much Mae missed him, he skipped over them. Instead, focusing on the mundane farm life that he and Freddie so longed for.

Sargent Baer visited each foxhole that afternoon. Talking with the men and sharing a little piece of something that felt like home. Just men talking about life, not Japs. He dropped into Finn's hole and patted him on the shoulder. When they left California, Baer was a mountain of a man, like a grizzly, so the men nicknamed him Griz. But now he just stood there like a large skeleton. The dysentery and lack of food on Guadalcanal left him much smaller. He was still a tall man, but he lacked the mass that made him look invincible. As Finn studied him for a moment and realized that Griz suddenly looked old. He was only in his early thirties, but now he seemed much older. The sparkle in his eyes was gone and replaced with the stare that comes from killing men in combat. The sad eyes that look through you into your soul.

"Holy shit. You boys had a feast from the looks of things," Griz said with a wide grin.

Freddie smiled, "We can make a meal out of just about anything."

Baer reached into his pocket and produced a flask. "Something to wash it down with?"

Finn smiled. "You old dog, what have you got there?"

Baer handed him the flask. "A little Kentucky windage to wash down your biscuits."

Finn took a swig from the flask and felt the burn and smokey flavor of bourbon. "Sarge, if I wasn't already married..."

Griz laughed. "You'd get nowhere with me. You're not my type. Too skinny, and you have a cock. I like em' bigger and no cock." He turned to Freddie. "Like DuMond. He's more my type. Ha, ha, ha."

Freddie frowned. "You're too hairy for me. Besides, my heart belongs to McGinn's sister Frances."

Griz leaned back and gave Freddie with a nod of approval. "Good for you DuMond. You make it home in one piece to marry her. That's a direct order."

Freddie smiled. "Yes, Sargeant."

Griz suddenly turned serious. "Listen to me. Stay alert tonight. We don't expect a sneak attack, but that's why they call it a sneak attack. We are going to move forward at first light and take that next ridge. It's bound to be bloody, so get your rest."

Finn nodded and understood. "Aye-aye, Griz." He started to hand the flask back, and Baer stopped him. Let's drink together. Get your cups."

Finn and Freddie poured the contents of their cups on the ground and Griz poured them each a shot. "McGinn do the toast. One of those Irish toasts."

Finn smiled, "May the lilt of Irish laughter, Lighten every load. May the mist of Irish magic, Shorten every road... And may all your friends remember all the favors you are owed. Slainte M'hath."

"Cheers," said Baer, and the three men drank.

When they emptied their cups, Baer grinned at Finn. "I don't owe you any favors McGinn.," he said with a chuckle.

"Well, we're not home yet, are we?"

Baer laughed again. "I suppose not... you two get some rest. I got a feeling tomorrow's going to be a hard day." Then he crawled out of the foxhole and tapped DuMond on the helmet. "Stay close to him and he'll get you home to meet that sister of his."

"I plan to," Freddie said with a smile.

Twenty–Two

ecember 1943

D Daisy pulled her collar up around her neck and tried to make her coat a little tighter. It was only December, but it already felt like winter. She was frozen to the bone from shoveling out her car to get to work.

Daisy had always lived in town, and everything was a quick walk away. But out on Howell Hill Road it was a long walk to everything. Alder had taught her to drive and bought a used 1936 Ford sedan. She liked the car, but a heater was an option and the previous owner decided not to buy that option. Alder had made a heater from sheet metal, but it barely took the chill off on a cold day and only served to irritate her on a frigid one. If it was cold enough, the heater would actually blow bits of frost inside the car.

She had made it a point to never complain to Alder about anything at home. As far as he was concerned, everything was great, and for the most part it was. She enjoyed working at the shoe shop and she was earning a good living. Her sister in laws watched the children and all the McGinn women rallied together. Cecelia, Mae and she were not McGinns by blood, but they had been so thoroughly welcomed that they felt like blood. Mary praised them of chided them as if they were hers and none of them ever minded it. She was so tough that they admired her for it.

As she pulled into the farm to pick Mary up for work, she saw Mary standing on the porch with her lunch-basket in her hands and a frown on her face. She hustled to the car and jumped in.

"We're going to be late." Mary said as she shut the door.

"Sorry. Ma. Took me a while to shovel out."

"Well, let's get going. We're probably not the only ones who'll be late."

Daisy threw the car into reverse and backed out with a small skid then shifted to first gear and they headed to town.

The car swayed a little on the snow-covered road, and Mary braced herself against the dash. "I'm not trying to be critical, but perhaps we could slow a trifle. More important to get there in one piece than to get there on time."

Daisy slowed a little, and the car immediately handled better. She looked at Mary all bundled up in multiple layers. "I'm sorry the heater isn't working so well."

Mary chuckled. "Sweetheart, when I was a girl, we only had a wagon and if there was enough snow, then a sleigh. Believe me. This car is like a summer day compared to ride in a sleigh. Did you know that it was a man from Massachusetts that wrote that song, *The One-Horse Open Sleigh*?"

Daisy crinkled her brow. "I don't think I know that one."

"You do. It's jingle bells."

"Oh, I never knew that was the real name. What about it?"

"I never cared for that song. Every sleigh ride was cold to me, and the seats in our sleigh were just wood planks. Not a very comfortable ride."

Daisy stared straight ahead just watching the road.

Mary was close enough to her, that she could tell when something was off. "Daisy. What's the matter?"

Daisy shrugged. "I'm just tired I think, and I miss Alder." She sniffled a little. "Joyce asks for him every day and the baby doesn't even know who he is."

"It's hard for all of us. But I feel for you the most. Allison has Melvin, Ceclia has Lewin, and Emma has Bill. But you are here alone. It's a lot to take on by yourself with the babies. That's why I'm always so proud that you are my daughter-in-law. That's why you're my favorite. But don't tell the others." Mary said with a wink.

That made Daisy laugh, and she imagined Mary saying that to Cecelia and Mae when they were alone. It may have been a joke. But it did make Daisy feel better.

"I do worry about the boys. I see those telegram cars around town, and it makes my heart sink that they might be coming to one of our houses."

Now Mary was quiet for a moment, then sighed. "I try with all my might to block it out, but it occupies every minute that my mind isn't busy. I think about Alvin and something foolish he used to say. He'd tell me *McGinns can't be killed by mortal means. They only die when they don't have any work left to do*."

Daisy shook her head. "Alder has said that to me before."

Mary chuckled. "It's dumb, but I use it to reassure myself that they'll all get home safely."

Daisy looked at Mary, then back to the road. "Alder is a mechanic, so I don't worry about him as much. But the others will all be in the thick of the war. John Roy was strong. Probably stronger than Joe and he's gone. I just can't bear to think of one of us getting a flag."

Mary picked at a snag on her coat and tried not to break. "I worry about them all so much. Even if they come back. They're never the same. When my brother Kevin was killed in the great war, it was awful. His boys were so small that they never really knew him."

"That's what worries me about the girls."

"As much as we missed Kevin, we were grateful that he didn't come back like some of the others with an arm missing or half their face. They were like the walking dead and sometimes they came back without a scratch like Winslow Hatch. But they carry warrior's wounds. Or at least that's what my father called it."

Daisy titled her head like she was trying to understand. "Warrior's wounds? I thought you said he didn't have a scratch."

Mary pulled again at the snag, trying to occupy her mind somewhere away from melancholy. "They see things. Horrific things. They do things that are unnatural. They live a regular life here. And there. They are killers. It leaves a mark that you can't see."

Daisy nodded. "Alder told me a story once that scared me half to death. But he made me swear to never tell it to anyone."

"So, why are you telling me?"

"I don't know. It's just something that I want to understand. But I can't wrap my mind around it."

Mary stopped picking at the sang and folder her hands in her lap. "I suspect I know what it is but tell me and it stays between us."

Daisy took a deep breath and paused. "Alder said that after Jim died, they captured a man from the Moreland farm. He said the man was the foreman like him. Doyle was his name."

"Yes, Delbert Doyle. What about him?"

"Alder said that they questioned him and when he told them about Jim and bootlegging operation, they were going to let him go, but his cousin pushed him into a ravine, and he died."

"Well, that makes more sense than the story they told me. I think I always knew what happened, but the way they said it was an accident and I wanted to believe that."

Daisy reached over and squeezed Mary's hand. "They did what they felt they had to. Aaron was worried that if they let him go, Doyle would have told the authorities."

Mary squeezed her hand back. "He wouldn't have had to. He would have told Parker Moreland, and Parker would have would have burned the whole mountain down to get revenge. They'd all be in prison or in the ground by now."

"God. Was Parker Moreland really that mean?"

Mary nodded. "Yeah. He was." She paused for a moment. "He wasn't always mean. But when his wife died, he changed overnight. She was beautiful, and he was very handsome. When you saw them in town, you knew that they were *somebody*."

"Mr. Moreland is not like that. He's the richest man I know, but he seems very down to earth."

"He is. He has a lot of money, but he spreads it around making jobs and more money. Parker made money and kept it. Like a miser. Just goes to show that you can't take it with you."

Daisy moved her hand back to the wheel. "Alder said that he tried to buy your farm."

"Ha! Alvin respected him, but he never liked him. Parker could have offered him top dollar and Alvin would have sold it at half price to anyone else in the world, just to spite him. Alvin admired how hard he worked to accumulate his fortune. He just didn't care for his tactics."

Daisy nodded. "Alder feels the same way. When Mr. Hartley down the road from you broke his back, Parker tried to buy his farm for a song. But Alder said that his father rallied all the locals, and they helped keep the farm going until Mr. Hartley recovered enough to do it on his own."

Mary smiled with pride. "That's true. Alvin would have worked day and night to keep that farm out of Parker's hands. God, he was stubborn... but that's one of the things I loved the most about him." Mary thought about Alvin and laughed aloud. "He told my father that we were going to have a baby and asked for my hand in marriage. My father was so mad that his face turned purple, and he threw Alvin out. He said he was sending me to a convent."

"That must have been terrifying. What did he do?"

Mary grinned. "Every morning and every evening he would come to the house and say, Arthur. I want to marry your daughter and I won't be denied. Then my father would close the door in his face. I'd watch from the window, and he'd always give me a wink or blow me a kiss." Mary paused in reflection. "This went on for nearly three weeks, and I think my father started to look forward to the encounter. He actually loved Alvin. He was just upset with him. One Sunday evening he came to the door and my mother was making a corned beef. When my father opened the door. He expected the same line, but Alvin sniffed the air and said, *good lord Arthur, the girl can wait, but I'd be forever in your debt for a small slice of that beef. We could call a truce today and resume hostilities again tomorrow.* My father stared at him for a moment and then burst into laughter and said, *come in and eat, then be on your way.*"

Daisy laughed. "Did he throw Alvin out after the meal?"

"No. Alvin was very clever. After dinner, they sat near the wood stove and Alvin had gotten it really hot. Then he passed him a flask of whiskey a couple of times and Dad was asleep. We went for a walk and when we returned, my father met us at the door. *Marry her*. That was all he said."

Daisy sat up straight in surprise. "Wait. What? That was it? Marry her."

"Well, he was never going to make me a nun. He just wanted Alvin to suffer. Alvin knew that, so that is why he was so persistent. It was just a matter of time." Mary looked down and grinned a little, but her eyes looked sad.

Daisy reached out and grabbed her hand again. "He sounds like quite a man."

"Well, he may have been a fool at times. But he was my fool and I still miss him."

Twenty–Three

December 1943

Finn grimaced and fought back tears as he was dragged across the ground. The pain was even worse than when he was shot. He didn't really know what had happened. They were moving through tall grass when a machine gun opened up and shot the guys up front to shit.

The last thing he had seen when the firing started was Griz spinning and falling like a giant top. He low crawled as fast as he could and found Griz shot through his gut and right shoulder. He was flailing on the ground, trying to get his gear off. "Mac! Help me. I'm FUBAR!"

Finn slid up beside him and plucked a bandage and sulfur packets from his pocket. He poured the sulfur into the wounds and plugged the holes with gauze.

"I have to get you to Doc Clinton. Do you think you can crawl?"

They were covered in a hail of dirt as a grenade went off to their right.

Griz tried to roll over and let out a muffled wail. "I don't think so Mac."

Finn pulled a morphine syrette and injected Griz in the thigh. "I'm going to give that about ten seconds and then we're out of here. They are getting way too close."

Griz nodded and seemed to relax a little. Finn knew it was times. He got to one knee and hauled Griz onto his shoulder and groaned as he stood. "Fuck Griz you're fat." He started forward and as he gained his balance, he started to move faster to the back. Every step brought a little gasp from Griz.

"Grenade!!!" he heard someone yell and turned his head to see a grenade hurtling through the air. He turned to move away from the blast and thought, *a damned Centerfielder.*

The blast went off beside him and felt himself momentarily off from his feet. He hit the ground with a thud and a crunch as all of his weight and all of Griz landed in a heap across a log. He gasped but couldn't catch his breath. He tried to breathe again, but his lungs wouldn't open. He tried to get Griz off from his back, but he was too weak to do it. *I'll just rest a minute,* he thought.

It was sometime later; he couldn't say how long that Freddie came and started dragging him to the rear. He could breathe again, but every breath was a struggle, and he had a strange sensation that he was drowning.

Freddie dragged him by his web gear. He had tried carrying him, but every step was agony for Finn. "Hang in there brother. We're almost to the Doc". He rounded a corner on the trail and they were back at the encampment from the previous night. "Doc! Doc! Help!"

Doc Clinton was kneeling over Sargent Baer applying new dressings. Baer was awake and bit a stick when the doc pulled the round from his shoulder. "You're going to be alright Griz. Get some sips of water. No gulping." Baer nodded and pulled the stick from his mouth.

Clinton turned to look at Finn. "Fred, where is he injured?"

Freddie shrugged, "His chest, I guess. But I didn't see any bullet holes. He fell across a log with Griz on his back."

Clinton cut Finn's shirt and saw that the whole right side of his chest was so bruised it was nearly black. He looked up at Finn. "Can you breathe?"

Finn gasped, "just."

"Okay, I need to drain the blood from your chest and you'll breath better."

Finn nodded and looked at his bruise and then looked away to his left.

"Mac, this is gonna' hurt."

Finn's eyes started to well with tears. "Fuckin' hurts now. Just do it."

Clinton pulled a small knife and a metal tube from his kit. He connected a tube from one end of the tube to a glass jar. He touched the blade to Finn's right side and sunk it between the ribs, making a deep incision. When he cut, Finn winced.

Freddie moved in and sat down behind Finn, holding him tightly so that he couldn't move and kept the shattered ribs exposed.

"Just hold on brother, it will be done in a minute."

Clinton slipped the tube into the slit and blood began to pour into the jar.

Finn groaned and started to weep as the blood drained from his chest. He wasn't sure if it was a relief that the pain was gone, or maybe he had just reached his breaking point.

"All done, all done, all done," Clinton whispered as he formed a seal around the tube. "You're going to a hospital ship, and you won't be back."

Finn shook his head, trying to see through the tears. "What are you saying?"

"Goin' home Mac." Clinton wiped his hands on a rag and looked at the blood filling the jar. "Him too," he said with a jerk of his thumb toward Griz.

Finn looked to see Baer grinning a little, leaned against a tree with a cigarette hanging from his mouth. "Freddie, drag me over to him."

"No!" said Clinton. "Don't drag him. We need a stretcher."

Finn grinned back. "Then drag his fat ass over here."

"Fuck you. Fat? I'm built like a man. Not a gangly teenage boy and I'll get myself over there."

Clinton shook his head. "Freddie, give me a hand so these two lovebirds can fawn over each other." They helped Griz to his feet and brought him to the tree that Finn was leaning against.

"You damned near crushed me under your manly frame."

"Thanks for breaking my fall Mac." He reached into his pocket and pulled a pack of cigarettes, "You want?"

"Yeah."

Doc Clinton stood with his hands on his hips and a look Finn had seen a thousand times from his mother. "Oh c'mon McGinn, you only got one lung workin'."

Griz lit a cigarette and placed it in the corner of Finn's mouth.

Finn took a puff and exhaled. "I'll only smoke half of one, then."

Freddie kneeled beside him. "Finn, I gotta get back to the line."

Finn nodded and started to tear up again. "I know. Thank you. Come marry my sister, so we can be brothers for real."

"See you when this is done." Freddie grabbed Finn around the neck and hugged him, then kissed the top of his head. "Thanks for keeping me safe."

Before Finn could say anything else, Freddie had jumped to his feet, grabbed his rifle and started running back to the front.

Griz leaned in toward Finn. "Your sister is going to be a lucky girl."

Finn nodded and pulled the cigarette from his mouth, crushing it out on the ground. "Yeah she is."

Mae sat on the front porch or their second-story apartment, drinking a cup of tea and reading a book. It was a three-season porch with large glass windows that made it quite comfortable, even in December as long as the sun was out. Today it was bright, and she could feel its warmth on her whole body. She had planted two dozen poinsettias in pots, on shelves, that ran the length of the porch. She had alternated reds and whites, and when stood at one end and looked down them it looked like a long candy cane.

The book she was reading was called Mildred Pierce. It was a story about a divorcee' in California trying to make a life for herself. She liked the book, but in her mind, she could only think of all the widows the war was making. In the book, Mildred's husband is a deadbeat, but these widows lost good men. A lot of good men and many of them had children. Some very small children.

She and Finn hadn't had children yet, so she wouldn't be in that boat, but she tried to imagine what the mothers would tell their child about why their father was never coming home. Just thinking about it made her feel melancholy.

She tried to keep reading, but didn't seem to like the story anymore. It brought her to a sad place, and she didn't like it. She laid the book on the little table and picked up her cup of tea, then walked to the windows. The street was coming alive with people walking by with bags from shopping and children playing in the little snow that had fallen so far. Kids were on the lawn of the library, building a snowman, and that made her smile. She loved the library, and it was practically across the street. It was a gray granite building with a copper dome. The inside was filled with beautiful wooden shelves full of books. The smell of old books always made her feel good and reminded her of reading in that library as a child.

The only thing that she didn't care for was the statue of the civil war soldier that had stood a silent post facing her porch windows in front of the building for decades. The statue had never bothered her until Finn went away. She worried that someday they would be looking at a statue of men from this war and Finn might be one of them. That made her feel sad all over again.

She shook her head and walked to the far end of the porch and leaned with her left eye closed so that she could look down the row of flowers. She smiled. *My living candy cane*, she thought and started to feel better.

Her bliss was broken by the sound of the doorbell ringing. He jumped and spilled a little of her tea. She couldn't see who was at the door but saw that it was only one man. She stood up and noticed a Western Union car parked at the end of the driveway. Her heart began to pound in her chest, and she found it hard to breathe. She tried to collect herself, and the doorbell rang again.

"Mae McGinn. Answer that door," she said aloud and exhaled, then headed to the stairs. The driver was an older man with wisps of curly hair that poked out from under his hat. He smiled and was missing a couple of teeth.

"I'm looking for Mae McGinn."

She held out a hand. "That's me."

He handed her a clipboard and she signed for the telegram. He took it back and gave her the envelope. "I hope it's good news, Ma'am. Merry Christmas."

She forced a small smile. "Merry Christmas to you too."

He turned and walked away. Mae looked around and shut the door, then ran back up the stairs to the apartment and locked herself in. She went to their bedroom and sat on the bed with the picture of Finn on the beach on the nightstand. She looked at him and smiled. "Don't send me bad news, Finn. I can't take it."

She took a deep breath, exhaled and ripped open the envelope. As she read it, she was in shock and collapsed on the bed and wept, then wailed. She sat back up and read it again, then picked up his picture and just stared. She held it as she went to the kitchen and called the McGinn farm.

Mary answered.

Mae sniffled. "Ma."

Mary was silent on the other end.

"He's coming home. He's hurt, but he's coming home." Then they both wept and Mae screamed with joy and kissed his picture over and over.

Twenty-Four

F inn sat at the bar in Slaughter's, staring at his beer. He didn't know how many it was. All he knew was that it wasn't enough. He had been having the same nightmares over and over. Japanese haunted his dreams. Every night it was the same thing, screaming *Banzai* and coming at him with fixed bayonets. One after one, they came. They all looked the same. Branches sticking out of their helmets and always with that same look. Eyes slanted down in blades of rage and the point of the bayonet gleaming like Excalibur ready to strike down Mordred at the end of Camelot. Always, the same dream. He killed them one after another and yet none of them ever touched him physically. It was his soul that they were wounding.

As a youth, he loved to fight. Beating another man was a thrill to him, but now all he wanted was peace. He remembered Winslow Hatch and how he has desired peace above all else, and now he finally understood. To kill a man leaves you with a chasm in your soul that you cannot fill by confession. Even if God forgives it, you are never quite able to forgive yourself.

Finn thought about his last days as a Marine. They were so hungry that they had eaten any piece of leather that they could find. Men had the seat of their trousers ripped out so that they could shit without having to drop their drawers due to dysentery and no one wanted to be killed with their pants down. They were a mob of walking skeletons and ran out of rations more than a week before victory.

During their march, they came across the remains of two paratroopers from the Army. They had been butchered. Their torsos hung in the air, suspended by their hands around a tree limb. From the waist down, they were nothing but butchered bones. They looked like so many half-butchered animals they had done on the farm that he had to check himself from vomiting.

The Japanese were so hungry that they were eating GIs. A week before, they had found dead Japs who had been eaten by other Japs and a few days later, a live Jap was caught with a pocket full of smoked fingers. He said that they ate it all, friend or foe. They were all so hungry.

He knew that Mae was getting frustrated with him, and he had only been home for two months. He had been gone two years, and that seemed like an eternity. But now every minute felt like it would never end. He was going to be starting back at Sampsons Cedar Mill in a few days, and that was fine with him. Old man Sampson started paying him a week earlier but

197

told him it was a hero's bonus and consider the first week on him. Who was Finn to argue with a week of pay without actually working for it?

He had to laugh at the change from the Mr. Sampson that called him a dim-witted doofus with horse shit in his ears. Now he was Finn this and Finn that. Anything you need, Finn? It actually felt good to be admired. Where do you think we should go, Finn? No one ever asked what he thought before the war.

Finn could feel the beer starting to hit him a little and was contemplating leaving until a couple of big mouths walked in. Kendall and Hugh Walker. They were younger, more like Alston's age, or maybe Patrick's. He couldn't remember for sure and didn't care. What he did remember was that he didn't like them. Their older brother Willis was Finn's age, and they had never been friendly. Willis was prone to loose talk about how tough he was, but Finn couldn't recall ever seeing him in a fight.

Even though he was drafted, Willis never left the United States. It turned out that he had a gift for accounting, so they made him a supply and logistics clerk. When Finn returned home, Willis was the one who processed him back into civilian life.

"Holy shit. Finn McGinn. Big time war hero to drunken shit heel," Kendall said with a laugh.

Finn looked at them for a long moment without looking away. "It's probably hard for two pissant fuck heads like you to understand since they don't give out medals for typing reports."

"What's that supposed to mean?" asked Hugh, and moved closer to Finn.

"Well, I'm sure your brother's paper cuts were deep, but probably didn't ever reach the level of a purple heart."

Kendall stepped behind Finn and now there was one on each side. "Are you saying he didn't do his part?"

"No. He did his part. Such as it was. Far, far better men than Willis Walker died, so assholes like you two have the freedom to run your mouths however you like." Finn clutched his mug tightly by the handle and drained the rest of his beer.

Hugh gave Finn a hard shove on his left shoulder. "Why don't we step outside, and we'll see who the hero is?"

Finn looked at him. Took a deep breath and exhaled. "Why wait?" He swung the heavy glass mug with as much force as he could muster and slammed it into the side of Hugh's head. The glass shattered and Hugh fell to the floor unconscious, with blood running down the side of his face.

Finn spun around as fast as he could and struck Kendall on the bridge of his nose with a hammer fist. Kendall staggered, dazed, as the blood began to flow. Before Kendall knew what was happening, Finn flipped him onto the floor and punched him in the face over and over until he was unconscious as well.

Hugh was starting to rouse back to life and Finn walked over to him and grabbed him by his collar. As he raised his right fist to punch him in the face, he heard the unmistakable sound of a shotgun breech snapping shut.

He heard a voice to his right. "God dammit Finn! Stop!" It was Big John Slaughter and both barrels of the gun were pointed at Finn. "You know I see you like my own brother, now listen to me!" He was called *Big John*, but he couldn't have been more than five foot eight. He had a son named John too, so instead of Junior, they just called the father Big John.

Finn looked at Hugh with blood flowing down his face and raised his right hand to punch him again.

Finn felt the cold barrels pressing on his ear. "STOP! Drop him McGinn!"

Somehow, the command voice that he had heard for the past two years got through and he dropped Hugh onto the floor with a loud thud as his head bounced.

Finn looked at the two Walker men beat to shit, bleeding all over Slaughter's floor.

"What do I owe you for the mug?" Finn asked.

Big John lowered the shotgun. "Nothing. Just don't come in here for a while. Next time, bring someone with you to keep you in line."

"I'll wait for Hatch."

John looked puzzled. "What the hell for? To throw you in jail?"

Finn shrugged. "It was self-defense."

John pointed to Hugh, "yeah on that guy, but the other guy didn't do anything except run his mouth reckless."

Finn shrugged again. "I wasn't going to wait to see if he was going to come to his brother's rescue."

Hugh started to wake and moaned on the floor. Slaughter poured a mug of water in his face, which caused him to choke and gag. "Get up Walker." Hugh shook his head to clear the cobwebs and felt the sting of his cut head. As he stood, he staggered a little and caught himself on the bar. "Where's Kenny?" he asked.

"Sleeping it off," Slaughter said, pointing to the bloody mess on the floor.

"What the hell happened?! McGinn. You did this!"

Finn started back toward Hugh and Big John stepped in. "Listen, big mouth. As far as I'm concerned, you shoved him first, so that was assault and self-defense on his part." Pointing at Finn. "McGinn struck your brother, so that was an assault. If you want to press the issue, you'll be arrested for assault and McGinn will be too and you two can finish his up in jail, but who'll be there to save you next time?"

Walker understood and nodded without speaking.

"Get your brother out of here. You guys have a lifetime ban. Don't come back."

"What about him?" Hugh asked, pointing at Finn.

"Two weeks."

Hugh stopped he stiffened. "Two weeks for him and lifetime for use. Why? That's bullshit."

"Well, I like him. And I don't like you. That's why."

Hugh slapped his brother lightly on the cheeks and woke him up enough to stand. As Kendall stood, he coughed and a mouth full of blood sprayed the front of Hugh's shirt.

"This place is a shit hole anyway," Hugh said as he walked past Big John.

"Careful now. Maybe you both assaulted Finn and me, and he was just protecting us."

Hugh shook his head and gave Big John a snarl, but decided he had probably talked enough for one night.

The next morning, Finn was about to pour a cup of coffee when he heard a rap on the door. He looked up to see Chief Hatch standing on his front step.

Finn sighed and opened the door. "Coffee Chief?"

Hatch looked at Finn with sad eyes. "No, let's take a ride."

"Am I under arrest?" Finn asked.

"You should be. But let's talk about that in the car."

Finn grabbed his coat and walked with the Chief to his car. Hatch opened the front door, so Finn figured he wasn't under arrest. Yet."

As they pulled out of the driveway, Hatch started driving toward Sparta. "You nearly killed the Walker boy. Did you know that?"

Finn looked out the window and felt a little ashamed. "Which one?"

"Kenny. He's in the hospital. You better hope your wife can help save him, because if he dies, it's going to go badly."

"They started it," Finn said and immediately felt embarrassed to sound like a petulant child explaining away his antics.

"I know. Big John told me everything. But if he dies, the court won't see it as a fair fight. They'll see a trained marine who beat an untrained man to death. Your medals won't keep them from charging you with manslaughter."

Finn felt ashamed of his actions. "I have no excuse, Chief. I haven't been right since I got back."

"I know. That's why Mae asked me to talk to you."

Finn sat up and looked at him. "Mae asked you?"

Hatch drove past the road to the McGinn farm and on past the Morelands. "Yes. She says she can't get through to you and maybe I could help you."

"You? How?"

"We share a common experience."

Finn looked at his shoes and fought back the memories of his time in the Pacific. Hatch pulled the car over next to an old wood's road. It was on the other side of Howell Hill from the Mountain House the McGinns owned. Finn knew it well. "Why are you stopping here?"

"Good spot."

"A good spot for what?"

"Killing yourself. That's what you are trying to do, right? You can't live with your deeds, so you are trying to drown them in booze."

Finn frowned. "No. It helps me to relax. That's all."

Hatch opened a thermos and poured a cup of coffee. "Want some?"

"No, thanks."

"Well, suit yourself." Hatch sipped at the coffee and Finn felt his stomach rumble when the sharp aroma hit his nose. It did smell good. "A few years ago, a guy from the Moreland Farm named Delbert Doyle got so drunk he fell seventy or so feet to his death. Did you hear about that?"

Finn avoided looking at Hatch in case guilt was literally written across his face. "Maybe I heard something about it. Why?"

"You have a lovely wife. Smart and beautiful."

"Thanks?" Finn said with some apprehension.

"Do you love her?"

"What the hell kind of question is that? Of course, I do."

"Okay then. Walk to the top of that hill and jump. It will only be about three or four seconds and you'll be dead. No more pain. No more torturing your wife with drinking. You can bury your demons in one action."

"I don't want to kill myself."

"I think you do, because you won't get help. Do you think you're the first dumb-fuck soldier who came home with the Warriors Wounds that shredded your soul? You're not."

"I can't talk about what I saw. What I did."

"You lived. You did what you needed to do."

"I did more than that."

Hatch put his coffee on the dash and turned to face Finn. "We all did. We all did things that made us ashamed. More than ashamed."

Finn could feel the hot sting of tears as they welled in his eyes.

Hatch reached over and grabbed him by the arm. "Look at me. Talk to me about it. It never leaves the car, or if we're not in the car, I'll never repeat it. You survived. You did what you had to do. From what I heard, the Japs did far worse to our boys."

Finn felt the tears fall down his cheeks. "They did," he croaked in a hoarse whisper.

"Will you let me help you? If not, head straight up that trail to the tippy top and jump. Save your wife the years of grief." Hatch stared at Finn, waiting for a response.

"The conversation never leaves us?"

"Never."

"Can I have some coffee?"

Hatch pulled a lunch box from the back seat and produced a cup. "Yes."

Twenty-Five

E arl looked at the menu, and his stomach grumbled. Everything sounded tasty and it generally was. The meats were fresh from the Moreland farm and the diner hired a local gal to cook when the old cook, Seymour Cote left to join the army. Her name was Renee Rancourt, and she was a lot easier on the eyes than old Seymour.

Earl ate at the diner more than he cared to, but the food was good, and he didn't have to cook it. Plus, he just liked the way Renee wore her apron. It reminded him of the war posters around town, of the woman in the red kerchief showing off her muscles.

Renee was much thinner than the woman in the poster, but she wore a kerchief too and he loved her brown eyes and tan skin. She had come from Canada soon after the war started and landed in Monroe where her brother had worked at the mill. When he left for war, she needed a way to make her own living and ended up here.

She had been a cook in a sugar shack during the late winters and Miss Rose, who loved all things maple syrup related, heard this, she hired her on the spot. It was a great choice and people raved about the food. Particularly the breakfasts. But Earl just loved her. She always smiled and always gave him a good-sized portion of whatever she was making. Maybe it was because he was so thin, or perhaps she just liked him too.

Once she had burned his pancakes a little by accident, but he was so enamored of her that he said he preferred them a little crispy and she continued to burn them whenever he ordered. Rather than tell her the truth, he simply changed to French Toast.

Tonight, was meatloaf night with mashed potato and brown gravy. It was one of Earl's favorites.

"What will it be Earl?" asked Ruth. She was always pleasant and stood up straight, ready to write his order down.

Earl pushed the menu across the counter. "Meatloaf special, black coffee and what is the pie today?"

"We have cherry and lemon meringue."

"Cherry please."

Ruth smiled and finished the order. "I'll get your coffee."

Earl watched Renee work. The food was already made, so she only needed to reheat it. She carved off a thick slice and laid it into a frying pan. *That's a generous portion*, he thought, *hope I have room for pie*.

She finished plating his order and glanced down the counter to see Ruth busy with another customer. There were no other orders, so she brought it herself. Earl began to panic a little in his chair. They had said the occasional hello, but not really too much past that and definitely not many topics other than food.

"Do you like meatloaf?" she asked.

Earl smiled and gulped at the same time. "I do actually. It's one of my favorites. I like the gravy too."

Renee refilled his coffee. "There's a family that comes in, the Wadleigh's and the father always orders a double order of the special. He has meatloaf, with a layer of potato and another meatloaf and another layer of potato, all piled high and covered in gravy. He calls it the Monroe Meatloaf Mountain. His kids love it. I've never seen children eat so much food. They can't get enough of it."

"I'm not sure I could eat a mountain myself." He said with a chuckle.

"Oh, what a ninny." Renee slapped her forehead. "I forgot your roll and butter."

He had noticed it was missing, but he didn't say anything. As absurd as it sounded, she was perfect in his mind, and he didn't want to see any flaws.

She returned with his rolls, and he had just stuffed a big pile of food into his mouth when she asked how the food was.

He smiled and mumbled great through teeth dripping with mashed potato and brown gravy. He quickly swallowed and wiped his mouth. "It's good. Really good."

Renee smiled and looked at him with soft brown eyes. "I hate that your brother hurt you."

Earl blushed and couldn't think of anything to say.

Renee realized she had made him uncomfortable and touched him on the hand. "I'm sorry. I didn't mean to make you feel awkward."

At first, he jumped a little at her touch, but he really liked her decided it was now or never. "Well, at least he left me one strong arm to hold a woman with."

She studied his right arm and realized how muscular it was. "That he did." She reached over and felt his biceps. "That he did," she said again. "I have to get back to work." She smiled and turned away.

Wait did she just wink at me? He thought. *I really like this woman.*

When he finished his meal, Ruth brought the pie over. He ate and tried to think of ways to hang around after he was done. It was slow enough he wasn't blocking any business, and he didn't really have anything very interesting to do. "Have you heard from Joe?" he asked.

Ruth grinned. "I get a letter every week. They are all quite boring. He doesn't seem to be doing anything except training. Alder and Alston said they had seen him in England, but all of his letters are postmarked from Maryland."

"Hmm. That seems odd," he remarked and took another bite of pie.

Ruth leaned in and whispered. "She likes you; you know."

Earl almost choked on his pie. "She does?" he whispered back.

"Yes. So, ask her out to a movie or something."

"I don't know what's playing."

"Geez Earl. It doesn't matter. Just ask her and watch whatever is there."

Earl tried to find something to say, but nothing came to mind.

Renee was turned to them, scrubbing down the cook-top. "Hey Renee! What was the name of the movie you wanted to see with Fred MacMurray and Barbara Stanwick?"

Reene turned and smiled. "Double Indemnity. My girlfriend said it was excellent."

"Yes, that's it. Double indemnity. Earl here, was talking about going to the movies, but he didn't know what was playing."

Ruth gazed at him with big eyes trying to will him to speak, and finally he mustered the courage.

"Renee. Would you like to come to the picture show with me after work?"

"I would love to. I walk to work, but if you wouldn't mind giving me a lift?...".

"If you don't mind an old truck, I'd be honored."

"Well, an old truck beats old shoes every day of the week and twice on Sundays."

Ruth smiled at Earl and opened her eyes wide then took his plate.

The thirty-four men that made up Operation Group Patrick sat in chairs watching the plan being told for the fourth time. It was very meticulous and included numerous contingency plans. They would jump into France ahead of the large-scale invasion and link up with the French underground. Their job was to secure a power plant and prevent the Germans from destroying infrastructure when the allies kicked their asses out of France.

Every man in the unit spoke some French, but Joe spoke it fluently, and was excited to see France. The land of his ancestors. At the end of the briefing, one of the men asked if they would be in civilian clothes to blend in?

The captain giving the briefing scowled. "You'll be in your US Army issued uniform. Beret and all."

"Why not go in disguise?" another man asked.

The captain scoffed. "Because we...are the fucking O.S.S . that's why."

The men erupted in laughter and cheers.

The captain chose to seize the moment. "We are better trained than any outfit in this war, good guys or bad guys. We have better weapons and you men are the most lethal weapon the U.S Army has. There'll be Jerries begging for a fucking flame thrower to burn them alive, rather than you face you hard sons-of-bitches!"

He let the frenzy die away a bit before he continued. "Know your job. Know your buddy's job. Know everybody's job by heart."

The men nodded and started to get up.

"One more thing. Come home alive. The point of this exercise is to make that German bastard die for HIS fatherland." This caused another cheer to go up. "Dismissed," he called as he left the podium.

Two nights later, they successfully jumped into France and made their way just south of a town named Argetan.

Operation Group Patrick was split into two groups. The main group of twenty-four men would assault the dam and hydroelectric station from the east side of the river, and a second team of two five-man fire teams would cross the river and below the dam and move up to cut off any route of escape to the west.

The whole operation reminded Joe of men that "drove deer" during hunting season at home. The bulk of the hunters would move through the woods in a line to a few waiting hunters along the wood roads. Joe never cared for that kind of hunting, but here it seemed to make complete sense. There were only four directions the Germans could go. In the water above the dam, over the wall below the dam, which would result in certain death. Or the east, west routes, both of which would be cut off by O.S.S. teams.

Joe was part of the west bank teams. They quietly slipped into row boats and crossed the river with muffled oars. The river had a healthy layer of fog below the dam that covered them perfectly. As they disembarked on the far bank, they could hear two men conversing in German. They were a two-man patrol walking the road to the dam.

Captain Cookson was leading the west bank teams and signaled to stop and get down, with a fist and a flat hand moving downward. He pointed at Joe and his friend Jim Garrison. He tapped the knife sheathed on his chest and then pointed to Joe and his left arm, then Jim and his right.

Although they didn't have a lot of hand signals, Joe knew what he meant. As the soldiers passed, Joe noticed that both of them had their weapons shouldered, so that decreased the risk of them getting off a shot. He and Jim emerged from the bushes behind them and crept up silently each with their M3 fighting knife in their hand. Joe was left-handed, so it actually made sense for him to assault the man on the left. When they were a few feet behind the soldiers, he glanced at Jim, and Jim nodded.

They sprang like cats and took both men from behind rather than slit their throats they slipped the long blades into the base of the skull at the top of the neck, rendering both men dead instantly. The operation was done with barely a sound, and they dragged the two bodies off from the road out of sight.

Cookson brought the rest of the men up. "Good work," he whispered.

Joe nodded and re-sheathed his blade. They moved up the edge of the road to muffle any footsteps. They were given thirty minutes to cross and get into position. They had made it in seventeen minutes, so now they waited. As they sat in their positions, they watched two soldiers sitting in chairs outside the plant entrance. One looked to be trying to catch a little sleep and the other one was looking out for vehicles not men on foot.

That's right, thought Joe, *just relax, nothing bad is going to happen tonight*. They waited and watched. A few minutes later, the action started. The sound of grenades on the east side of the river was followed by an eruption of gunfire. The sleeping soldier jumped to his feet in time to be shot in the chest and the other German was dead a second after the first explosion.

"Keep your cover!" shouted Cookson. So, they waited all aiming for the door.

It didn't take long until Germans tried to flee. The first group exited and ran for the armored vehicle parked to the left of the station. A series of quick bursts left the three men dead.

Screams and gunfire filled the air. They were yelling in German, but soon that was silenced. A few more Germans tried to flee but met the same fate as their comrades. Eventually, the gunfire became more sporadic.

They heard a man call out from inside the plant. "Surprise! Kill!"

"And Vanish!" Cookson called out in reply. It was the O.S.S. motto, and it meant that the job was done. They had taken the plant. One man from the east team was hit with a grazing wound, but otherwise no casualties. The Germans lost eighteen men. Twenty if they counted to two on the road.

"It's a good piece of work. Now let's hold it," said Cookson.

They cleared the dead Germans and set up defensive positions. The Germans never returned however, because in the morning, the landings started on the beaches of Normandy, and they had bigger problems to confront.

Twenty–Six

June 6, 1944

Alston stood on the deck of the USS Bayfield waiting for his turn to board the Higgins boat, that laid tossing alongside the ship. They had already made multiple trips to Utah and the boat was half filled with wounded men. They had rigged stretchers pulled on ropes to bring the wounded to the main deck. Teams of sailors transferred wounded men to hand stretchers and they were laid out on the deck, waiting their turn for medical attention. Their green uniforms now torn and saturated with blood from one wound or another.

He tried not to think about it and instead turned his mind to prayer. He thought about saying the Our Father or Hail Mary prayers, but instead he focused on a personal request. *God, please bring us victory today. Our cause is just. Keep my family safe, especially my mother. She had bared enough pain for one lifetime and please bring me home to them.*

He doubted it was enough of a prayer, but that was all he had. He glanced around and saw other men praying as well. *God is probably overwhelmed with prayers today*, he thought. *I hope he heard mine.*

He could see the last of the wounded coming aboard and rechecked his gear. He rechecked his Browning Automatic Rifle one more time and made sure the safety was on. It was one thing to kill the enemy, but he couldn't live with himself if a misfire wounded one of his buddies.

A great burly sailor they called the Boson's mate, yelled to the waiting troops. "Gentlemen! Disembark! God bless you!" Alston didn't know what a Boson was but he seemed to be the boss of everyone on deck.

The mass of men started over the side down the thick rope ladder into the awaiting boat. As he climbed over the edge, he could see the bloody deck of the boat and somehow it seemed like a floating coffin. His BAR made it awkward to climb and the barrel kept slapping him in the side of the helmet. It didn't hurt, but it was annoying, and he didn't dare loosen his grip for fear of falling onto the men below, so he just kept moving.

When he reached the deck of the Higgins boat, he tried to find a place near the front to get out of the way of other men loading. It wasn't hard because no one wanted to be in the front line for disembarking, because they were the most vulnerable when the door opened.

The whole operation only took a few minutes to load the boat and driver started off. Standing on the deck of the ship,

217

he could only hear the massive pounding of the great guns barraging the German positions. But down here there were new sounds. Sounds of the diesel engine roaring behind him. The sound of waves slapping the wooden sides of the boat beside him and the sounds of prayers and retching in the boat with him.

As they approached the shore, he could see tracer rounds flying by. They zipped by like a thousand shooting stars trying to escape the coast. The sound of small arms fire now started to drown out the big guns and he could hear men yelling at the beach.

His heart was pounding in his chest, and he found it difficult to fill his lungs. He made the sign of the cross for one last moment of prayer. *Da, if you're listening, give me strength. If not. I'll see you in a few minutes.* Then he moved the Browning from his shoulder in front of him and snapped the safety to *fire and* made the sign of the cross again.

"Make that prayer a good one Al," said a voice beside him. It was Hank Golden. A buddy from all the way back in boot camp. Golden was a tall, Jewish guy from the north shore of Boston. Alston liked him and they shared a love of the Red Sox.

"Are the sox playing today?" Alston asked to break the tension in his mind.

"Nah. Travel Day. Fucking Yankees tomorrow." Golden turned and spat on the deck.

"Thirty seconds!" the driver yelled.

Alston took a deep breath and exhaled looking at Hank.

Golden stuffed a huge wad of chewing tobacco into his cheek and gave Alston a wink. "When this is over. We'll catch a sox game together. Deal?"

Alston nodded and gave a nervous laugh. "Deal." It made him feel better to think about a good thing in that moment.

"Ten seconds!" bellowed the driver.

Now the gunfire was nearly deafening, and he could hear bullets hitting the seven-foot bow door in front of him in a series of pings.

"Run fast McGinn!" Golden shouted and got into a ready position. The door started to open and the few men in front of him jumped out the side openings as soon as there was enough room for a man to escape.

When the door splashed down in front of him he was about to sprint forward when his left hand felt as though it had burst into flames and his side had caught fire as well. The force of the bullet knocked him backward and oncoming men shoved him aside to escape their floating coffin. He saw Hank running forward and as he cleared the deck he stumbled and started slogging through the surf. A second later his head snapped back and he fell backward into the water.

Alston struggled to keep his feet and another soldier grabbed his BAR.

"Give it to me McGinn!" the soldier shouted and ripped it from his hands leaving his M-1 with Alston. When he tried to grip the weapon, it fell to the deck and Alston examined his hand to see how he could have dropped it. His first and second fingers on his right hand were hanging perpendicular to the rest of his hand. As he raised his hand to look at it, he felt a fierce yank and he was on his back laying across a dead man.

"Stay down!" someone yelled, and the last man left the boat.

The door came up in a ponderous ascent, then closed completely. He could hear the screams of dying men and the pings of bullets hitting the bow door again. The big diesel engine roared into action and the boat slid backward, turned and was headed back to the Bayfield.

The boat moved much faster without so many men aboard but the tossing in the waves seemed much worse. One of the boat's gunners started sorting the wounded. He opened a bag and pulled out a handful of bandages. He knelt beside Alston and rolled him onto his left side.

"Through and through. Might have got your liver though." He pulled Alston's shirt up and poured sulfur on the wounds then slapped the bandaged to the bloody holes. When he felt satisfied, he turned to Alston's hand. "Let me see."

Alston held up his hand and the sight of his fingers dangling made him feel a little cold, and a bit queasy.

"I'm no doctor, but I'd say your pitching career is fucked."

Alston tried to smile at him but felt faint as he straitened the dangling fingers and wrapped them tightly in a bandage. He grabbed Alston by the wrist and moved his hand up near his ear.

"Hold this here as long as you can. It will help stop the bleeding."

"I'm so cold." Alston said in a voice al little above a whisper.

"You might be going into shock, Lay back."

Alston suddenly thought, this guy sure seems like a doctor. He laid on the bloody heaving deck and the gunned picked his feet up and rested them on top of one of the dead men. He could see Alston's surprise at placing his feet on another man.

"He won't mind it. He's gone."

Alston looked at the other bodies around him, then back at the gunner.

"They're gone too. You're the only one still with us. Rest now we're almost there."

Alston felt weak and just nodded. Then closed his eyes for moment.

When he woke up, he was on the deck with the other wounded. He didn't remember the trip up the side, but maybe that was for the best. When he has watched the operation earlier, it didn't seem very comfortable.

A sailor with a bloody uniform was walking among the wounded, conducting a triage of those laid out on the deck. *That must be the doctor*, he thought. When he reached Alston, he peeled back the blood-soaked bandage. He turned to a corpsman behind him and said, "Let's get him prepped for surgery. Make him number three on the list."

"Aye, aye sir," replied the corpsman who motioned to a couple of sailors who came with a stretcher.

The doctor peeled back the bloody gauze on the bandaged hand, and patted Alston on the shoulder. "I'll look at the hand when we get you down there. You're going to be alright."

Alston nodded and waited for the stretcher.

That evening he awoke in the sick bay. His hand was throbbing, but he didn't mind it too much. He was just happy to be alive. He thought of Hank and all the others lying dead on the beach and his heart ached. He looked around the room and tried to sit up. When he did, he felt a pain in his side that felt like he had been kicked by a horse and made an audible wince.

A corpsman was nearby and ran to his bedside in a panic. He was a tall skinny kid and, in some ways, reminded him of his brother Sean, all arms and legs. "Stay layin' down. You don't want to rip your stitches. How are you feeling?"

Alston had to think about that for a moment. He still felt like he was in a fog. "Tired. Hungry I guess... and thirsty."

The kid smiled. "Let me get you some water to help celebrate. It's not champagne, but you'll have to make do."

Alston was puzzled. "Celebrate what?"

"We've secured the beaches. We took Normandy."

Alston grinned. "That's positive, I guess. It was pretty bad on the way in. Did we lose many men?"

The boy's expression instantly turned to one of sadness. "A couple thousand. Maybe more and twice that wounded."

Two thousand men dead in one day. That would be like the whole town of Monroe dying in a single afternoon. The very thought of it made Alston melancholy. "There'll be a lot a families getting telegrams tomorrow. God help them."

The doctor came walking through the ward and stopped at Alton's bed.

"I told you, you'll be alright. I was able to contain the bleeding from the bullet that passed through your liver. Luckily it didn't hit any major blood vessels. But you'll be sore and weak for a while."

Alston nodded in understanding and held up his hand. "What about this?"

The doctor was more serious than he had been previously. "That's another story. The bullet struck the knuckle of your middle finger and that couldn't be salvaged. Your index finger is broken in multiple places, but I believe that you will still be able to keep it. I can't say if you'll ever be able to bend it again. At least it's still on there."

Alston looked at his left hand and tried to flex his middle finger to see what it would look like.

"The good news is that your Army days are done."

Alston didn't know if that was good news or not, but the thought of going home, made his heart feel a little more at ease.

J.E. MCCARTHY

Twenty–Seven

Mae laid in bed watching Finn sleep. He looked tense even when he slept, but at least it was a night without nightmares. She remembered how happy she was when she got word that he was coming home. She could have walked the ten miles to town on clouds she felt so light. He was strong and handsome and always full of life.

When she met him at the train station, he looked so impressive in his uniform that her heart swelled with pride. He had ribbons galore and a box with two medals for valor. His face was still handsome, but he was thin. Rail thin. He had sunken eyes and the sparkle that had melted her heart was gone. They were sad and lifeless. He was excited to see her and kissed her face over and over as he squeezed her. But when he released her, he smiled at her with those sad eyes. He looked like a living contradiction. Great toothy smile with eyes that looked like they might burst into flood, at the slightest hurt.

The first days were happy, and they made love every night. It was like being newlyweds again. She would go to sleep in his arms and then wake to an empty bed. At first, she was nervous that he was gone, and would get up to search for him. But he was always in the same place. Sitting on the porch with a bottle of whiskey and a pack of cigarettes. Just sitting. Staring at nothing completely oblivious to her presence.

"Finn," she whispered, and he jumped like a bomb had gone off beside him.

He clutched at his chest. "Wow! You gave me a hell of a start."

She looked at him and smiled. "Come to bed, Love."

He smiled back and nodded. "In a bit. I'm going to finish this smoke and I'll be in."

She went up and waited. And waited and then fell asleep. Some nights he came back to bed and other nights she found him passed out in a chair on the porch. The McGinns had all been drinkers, but this was way too much to be healthy.

This had gone on for the whole summer, and in her frustration, she reached out to Father Quinn and Chief Hatch. Finn met with Father Quinn, but that didn't seem to have any effect. When he met with Hatch little by little, he seemed to come back to life.

It was after one of those meetings that she finally worked up the nerve to ask him about the war.

They were sitting on the porch watching the sunset together. It was a pink and blue sky, and she saw Finn smile at the beauty of it all.

"Finn. Can I ask you a question?" she said softly.

"Of course, sweetheart," he said and quickly realized he had opened himself up for questions he didn't want to answer, but smiled, anyway.

"What do you dream about that keeps you up at night? Every night it's the same. Please tell me."

At first, he looked angry, but then he softened. "This is between husband and wife. No others ever. Do you understand me?"

She nodded.

"I'm serious. No one. Not my brothers or anyone else, and especially never my mother."

She nodded again.

"Swear it."

"For God's sake Finn, do I need to get a bible? I won't say a word."

He looked at her and then lit a cigarette and looked back at the sunset.

"We were on this ridge that we had taken from the Japs. We had four prisoners and one of them was from San Francisco and spoke perfect English. The other three were wounded and would have probably died from their wounds. The guy that spoke English didn't have a scratch. When Lieutenant Schwartz finally made his way to our position, he said, *no prisoners* and ordered me to have them shot."

She gasped a little in disbelief, and Finn paused for a second and started on.

"I couldn't order my men to do it, so I did, and the English speaker begged to be shot first. So, I shot him and then the others. When I turned to Schwartz, he was smiling."

Finn paused again. Took a long drag of his cigarette and exhaled. "Fucking Schwartz...later that evening we were preparing our positions to attack in the morning and Schwartz decides he needs to see the lay of the land for himself."

Finn looked at the floor and shook his head. "I advised him to use the intel the recon guys had gathered, but he insisted on looking for himself. He walked to the top of the berm and put a pair of binoculars to his eyes. He looked around and said *I can't see shit*. Then, a second later, the back of his head exploded from a sniper round. He turned and looked at me and was still standing. It was horrifying. He staggered toward me, and another round rang out and struck him in the chest, knocking him to the ground and he still looked at me with unbelieving eyes, but he was already dead. And he had that same damned smile on his face."

Finn flicked the cigarette on the floor and took another drag. "Everyone was yelling for a medic, and I said *shut the fuck up! Get me his personal effects and drag his ass to the rear. He's not for saving.* The whole back of his head was gone." He paused and shook his head like somehow, he could shake the vision from his mind.

"That night we tried to get some sleep, in short shifts, but we knew they would be coming. That was their favorite tactic to attack at night. When the attack came, we could hear them running up the hill toward us screaming *Banzai*! And all other manner of Japanese cursing too. We had cases of grenades and we just kept throwing them. Just a chorus of thunder and screams, a dozen yards down the hill."

He paused again to smoke and snuck a glimpse of Mae. She had a look of sadness and horror all at the same time.

"Then Reese who could speak Japanese said that they were retreating. *Fuck that! Call them back*, I said, *or we'll have to fight these sons of bitches tomorrow*. Reese stared bellowing in Japanese and yelled Charge! Over and over...and they came back. When we were nearly out of grenades, they finally made it to our side of the hill and were cut to ribbons. It wasn't war, it was slaughter. Then in the morning we looked out at hundreds of dead and dying Japs. They had abandoned their position on the opposite hill and moved further into the jungle. We fixed bayonets and methodically made sure that no prisoners would be taken. At the end of that day, the Colonel assessed the scene and told me that he was putting me up for a commendation. A medal. We killed so many men... and I won a medal. A fucking medal."

Mae slid toward him and wrapped her arms around him. She hadn't realized that the last few sentences were said through tears, and she squeezed him.

"You asked what I dream of? I dream of that night only I keep shooting and they keep coming. The English-speaking Jap and Schwartz with his stupid grin and blown-up head. They just keep coming. They won't let me rest."

She held him tighter. "At least you came home to me."

"It's not the killing that bothers me, but the way that I did it. I shot unarmed men in the head. We stabbed dying men through the heart. Some guys laughed and others smashed the gold teeth out of corpses. Some things we did worse than that. But those things are never being said to you. Father Quinn gave me absolution, but I haven't figured out how to give myself absolution."

She laid her head on his shoulder. "You never have to explain to me. I'm just glad that you are home with me."

He sat up and wrapped his arm around her. "Maybe someday those dreams will leave me be."

The next morning was a Saturday, and Chief Hatch picked him up for their weekly check-in meeting. "Good morning," he said and handed Finn a blueberry muffin. "The missus just made em', so they're still warm."

Finn bit into the muffin and the tang of blueberry, with the saltiness of melted butter was like heaven in his mouth. "Wow. That woman can bake."

Hatch laughed and patted his large belly. "Did you ever doubt it?"

Finn laughed and took another bite, then he looked at Hatch. "I told her about the attack on the ridge."

Hatch paused. "How'd she take it?"

"She was shocked. She felt bad for me. But she's just happy I'm home."

"Well, sometimes that's all we need. Just someone who cares for us more than we care for ourselves."

Finn took another bite and savored the muffin. "Is that why you reached out to me? You care about me?"

Hatch looked at Finn and grinned. "No, I don't give a shit a about you. But I figure it's easier than arresting you for disturbing my peace."

Finn laughed and went back to his muffin.

Hatch grew serious and stared ahead as he drove. "Finn. I have a confession that I hope please stays between you and me."

Finn put down the muffin. "Yeah, of course, Chief."

"I knew Hub killed your brother. I knew it in my heart. But I also knew I couldn't prove it and Parker Moreland would have hired a team of New York lawyers to drag your family into that courthouse for a year. And he probably would still have walked."

Finn was a little shocked, but not as much as he had imagined he should be. "Why tell me now?"

"I don't know. I feel like if I had arrested him and Doyle, maybe Doyle would have spilled the beans on Hub." He thought for a long moment. "Maybe Parker would still be alive. He was an asshole for sure. But he was my friend."

"Huh, with friends like that who needs enemies?"

Hatch shrugged. "Believe what you want. He wasn't always like that. When we were young, he was fun. He loved, and I

231

mean loved his wife. She was his whole life and I remember how happy he was when Hub was born. He beamed and handed out cigars to everyone. Good ones too. Cubans."

Finn was a little taken aback. "Wow. I can't even imagine it."

"We went *out on the town* and had some drinks. Then he went home to tend to the farm and bring some things back for his wife." Hatch paused for a long time and Finn became restless with waiting. "When he got back to the hospital in the morning, she was dead. Bled to death out her lady parts. Hemorrhage, they called it."

"Wow, and with Hub not even one day old?"

Hatch nodded. "He changed. He changed that very day and over time the anger built, but he never let it out. Instead, he poured his rage into the acquisition of property. Now he bought property the regular way, but he preferred to get it through desperation. Where somehow, he could assert his dominance over you."

Finn looked at Hatch and forced a smile. "I appreciate you telling me that, Chief. But I suspect the only outcome that would have happened is the one that did. Hub went to prison, and he's been ruined."

Hatch looked at the road as he drove. "I do miss my friend sometimes. They are getting fewer and fewer as I get older."

"Well, I consider you a friend, a damned good friend."

Twenty–Eight

Patrick sat with a stiff posture outside of the Commander Evans' office at Pearl. It was something akin to standing at attention in a seated position. He was up for a promotion to Chief Petty Officer, but it required staying in for another two years. He liked the Navy. He liked the structure, and he had become accustomed to routines.

In many ways it wasn't that different from life on the farm with the repetitiveness of chores, but the one thing he was growing tired of was submarine life. They were at sea for weeks, which meant most of his time was beneath the ocean breathing recycled air, ripe with diesel fumes, body odor, feet and aging canvas. They laid on cots that were over ten years old and no matter how he turned, he found it hard to get comfortable.

As he sat waiting, he realized that he was uncomfortable right now. The hard chair and the rigid posture combined to make his boney ass sore. He tried to shift his weight a little from side to side. He wanted to stand, but he didn't want to pace around the office in a nervous sweat. He tried to think of anything and then settled on the farm. What would they be doing right now? It was summer. Would Sean be cutting hay? Would they have any tomatoes yet? If it was warm enough, they might have tomatoes already. He wondered if Sean was doing a good job of maintaining the equipment.

"McGinn. The Commander will see you now."

Patrick jumped to his feet and entered the commander's office. "Sir, Seaman First Class McGinn reporting as ordered, Sir."

Commander Evans was a younger man. Definitely under forty. As he sat behind his desk reading papers from a file with Patrick's name on it, he noticed the massive class ring from Annapolis on his right ring finger and how funny it looked compared to the scrawny band that passed for his wedding ring. It made Sean wonder who he was actually married to.

"At ease McGinn. Have a seat."

Patrick exhaled and sat in the chair facing Evans.

Evans looked up. "Excellent career McGinn."

Patrick grinned a little. "Thank you, sir."

"Commander Hendricks says that you are one of the finest men ever to sail with him. That's high praise indeed. He's so tough he doesn't even buy his own kids Christmas presents." Evans chuckled and Patrick smiled but didn't laugh himself. Even though Evans was being cordial, he still felt like he might burst from anticipation.

Evans put all the papers away, folded his hands in front of him, and looked into Patrick's eyes. "McGinn, you have served on every patrol the Narwhal had in this war. I would like to promote you to chief, but there's no spot on the boat for another chief. I could put you on another boat, but that may be a while too."

Patrick's heart sunk a little. He really didn't want to be on a boat anymore. At least not for a while. He just wanted to be on land. "Sir, may I speak?"

"Yes. Of course. Speak freely man."

Patric inhaled and let out a deep breath. "Well Sir. I'd rather not be on a boat for a bit. I'm not afraid, and if that's my only option, I'll go willingly."

"Really. Most people want to go home about now. Not too many stick around a second longer than they have to."

"Yes, Sir. Most of the boat has cycled out in my time. I want to stay in, but I'd like to be on land if I can."

Evans nodded. "I appreciate your honesty. But I don't really have a lot on land here at Pearl." He looked at a list on his desk. "Huh. This might work. I assume you were on the boat when it went to Mare Island in California?"

"I was, sir."

"We have an anti-submarine school there. It is a more of a logistics position, but you would coordinate the moving sailors through classes and probably teach a few yourself. More hands-on teaching than classroom. Something like that appeal to you?"

Patrick's heart began to race. *Appeal to me*, he thought, *who would I have to kill to get it?* "Yes sir. It would appeal to me very much."

"Okay. I can't just give it to you. But I have a buddy from Annapolis in charge of the base there and they don't get many applicants with a Bronze Star. That should count for something. Get a good night's rest and report here tomorrow at 0900. I'll see what I can do."

Patrick smiled openly and jumped to attention. "Thank you, sir." He snapped a crisp salute and Evans stood and returned it.

"Thank you, McGinn. Dismissed."

Patrick walked outside and around the corner of the building then let out a giant, "whoop!" It was more than he could have imagined. He had been writing to Li when he was in port, but their mail was heavily scrutinized, so it was always a lot of small talk. Even though she was Chinese, he didn't trust people not to hassle her if they thought she was some kind of spy.

He walked as if he didn't have a care in the world. The Hawaiian sun felt good on his face, and he soaked it in like a sponge expanding with water. He could picture walking through San Francisco with Li and riding on cable cars around the city. He could imagine holding her hand and finally kissing her. It felt good to dream.

His dream was broken by an image of his mother's face. A mask of disappointment. Alston's look of hurt and anger and anyone else who felt betrayed that he wouldn't be home for another two years. But he loved his Navy life, and he wasn't certain that he would ever return at all. If he did, he hoped to have a Chinese wife. To him she looked like porcelain perfection. The image in his minds of Li was shattered by a shipmate calling his name.

"Pat, you goofy bastard! You'll burn your eyes out looking at the sun." It was Crocker. One of the cooks from the boat. His name was Ed, but everybody called him "Betty" because he was a cook with the last name Crocker. Eventually is was shortened to "Betts" and he didn't seem to mind it as much.

"I'm not looking at the sun Betts. I'm just soaking it in."

"Oh. Well, I'm heading to movies after chow. They have a movie called *Summer Storm* playing. In the poster, the dame's tits are practically falling out. Can you believe it?"

"What's it about?" asked Patrick.

Betts frowned. "How should I know? Tits I hope."

Patrick laughed. "They don't make movies about tits. At least not that they'd play on base."

"Well, a storm in the summer, then. I don't know. You comin' or not?"

"Probably. I need to write some letters first."

Betts shook his head. "For the love of Christ McGinn. You have all weekend for that. Come out with me. We'll find something to celebrate...I know. Let's celebrate being on land and not breathing recycled air for weeks at a time."

Pat smiled and nodded. "Now that I can celebrate."

"Good. I know just the place." Betts led him across the base and landed at the Anchors Away bar. It was the first place he had a drink in Pearl Harbor.

"Nice choice," Patrick said with a chuckle.

"You know this place?"

"Yeah. Good whiskey here."

They walked inside and found a place at the end of the bar. It was bright, like Patrick remembered it.

Betts smiled. "Okay then. We'll start with a little *water of life,* and then have some beers."

"Not too many. I have to report to the Commander again in the morning."

"For what?"

"Promotion opportunities."

"Well, you son-of-a-bitch. You're re-upping."

Patrick grinned. "Yeah."

Crocker shook his head. "Why? This war will be done soon. You can go home and have a regular life."

"I like my Navy life."

Crocker laughed. "You can have it. I'm out the door the minute they say I'm free and I'm never making shit-on-a-shingle again for the rest of my life."

Now Patrick laughed. "I actually like SOS."

Crocker shook his head in disgust.

The bartender made his way to serve them and stopped. He looked at Patrick. "I know you. The guy from Maine right?"

Pat smiled. "Yes. That's right. You have one hell of a memory."

"They still married?"

Patrick nodded. "Yeah. He's in Europe now. Still alive, as far as I know. But he's tough. I mean really tough. He'll be fine."

The bartender nodded. "Tough helps. I've seen a lot of tough Marines come through here on their way to the islands and come back like walking skeletons. It's sad."

Pat felt a little melancholy. "My brother Finn was one. He's home now. Got shot a couple of times. My Ma says he's in a bad space and can't get out of it."

The bartender looked at Pat and Betts. "A lot of em' are... Whiskey?"

Betts smiled. "Sure. Irish if you got it in honor of Mr. McGinn here," and shoved Pat in the arm.

The bartender produced three shot glasses and a bottle. He poured them each a full shot. "The first one's on me. Let's drink to your brother. May he and the rest of those guys find peace. Cheers."

"Slainte M'hath." Pat whispered and drank his shot.

That night Patrick laid in his cot thinking about Finn and the difference between sending a ship to the bottom of the Pacific and blowing a man's head off. How do they ever get right?

Sinking a ship is anonymous. You don't even see it go down. Somebody else just tells you it sank, and you cheer. The guys on the ground see it, hear it, feel it.

He missed his brother.

Twenty–Nine

December 1944

Alston sat looking out of the window. Maine was at its dreariest. The trees were all bare. The ground was covered with brown leaves, and everything looked incredibly stark. No brightly colored leaves of the fall and no snow yet to brighten everyone's mood. In spite of all that, he still thought that it might be the most beautiful landscape he had ever seen. He was home.

He checked his watch for the twentieth time this hour and realized that he was only ten minutes from Watertown. Along the way, he had seen numerous GIs get off the train and run into the arms of a wife or sweetheart. It made him a little sad. He'd be meeting family. It didn't quite have the same appeal, but he would be happy to be home.

The closer he got, the more familiar all the landmarks seemed to be. He started to think that he recognized specific trees in a forest. The anticipation was making him a little loopy. Then they crossed over the trestle on the Black River, and he could see the station. Then the platform, and covering the entire end of the platform closest to him were McGinns. He pressed his face to the glass and peered down the line. They were all there. It made his heart leap with joy.

He stood up and straightened his uniform. He smoothed out the jacket and turned to an old man sitting across the aisle watching him.

"How do I look?" he asked.

The old man eyed him up and down. "You'll pass inspection." He grinned and gave Alston a wink.

"Thank you, sir."

The old man chuckled. "I see they got your driving finger."

Alston looked down at the stump of his former middle finger. "My driving finger?"

"Yeah, who will people from away know what you think of them?" He held his hand up and flipped him the middle finger, then roared with laughter. He had no teeth and his heavy white stubble made Alston think of a circus clown, and that made him laugh.

The train began to slow, and the whistle blew. It was the best sound Alston had ever heard in his whole life.

The passengers shuffled forward like cattle being herded through a chute and took his place in line. He cleared the car door and immediately felt the cold Maine air slap him in the face, like it was saying, *welcome home*. His eyes adjusted to the low December sun and the first face he saw was his mother's.

Mary stood smiling as if she might burst. When he cleared the last step, he dropped his bag and scooped her up in his arms, twirling her around and around.

"Put me down. It's not dignified."

He released her and looked her in the eyes. "I missed you Ma."

She fought back tears and shook her head. "Don't even get me started on what you boys have put us all through."

He chuckled. "I'm sure it was far worse than being shot at."

"Don't be smart with me Alston McGinn," she said and gave him that look. The look that said, *don't tread there* without even speaking.

He laughed. "I'm just teasing Ma. I'm sure it's been hard everywhere."

Finn stepped up and shook his hand. He looked much older now. The vibrant youth was gone, and now a shell stood before him. Lewin hobbled over, using a cane. His knee still didn't flex well, but otherwise he looked the same.

He hugged his sisters and sisters-in-law and it felt good to be back with his family. He felt safe.

When they reached the farm, Sean met them on the porch. "Welcome home big brother."

Alston smiled and couldn't believe his eyes. When he left, Sean was a boy and now somehow, he had become a man.

Sean smiled from ear to ear. "I have a surprise for you."

"What is it?" Alston asked, but he could already smell the aroma of roasting meat.

"This," Sean said and opened the lid of his cooker. It was the front quarter of a deer covered in bacon.

Alston sniffed the air. "You stole my recipe," he said with a chuckle.

Sean looked skeptical. "Pat said he came up with the bacon on the meat." Sean turned the meat and handed Alston a mason jar.

"Huh. That was my idea, because he kept drying the meat out." Alston sniffed at the jar. He could smell the alcohol and pulled away from the jar. "Poteen?"

Sean nodded. "Yeah, my first attempt. I've been adding a lot of lemons, so it's more like lemonade."

"Smells like piss." Alston said with a frown.

"Tastes like piss too." It was Finn. He stepped up and looked at Alston's hand. "I don't know if that's fortunate or unfortunate. It got you home, but your right hand would have been a lot less inconvenient, being a lefty."

Alston chuckled. "You're not kidding. You ever tried to eat or write or even wipe your ass with your opposite hand? It's not easy."

Finn nodded in agreement. "Can't imagine it would be."

"How are you doing? People said you roughed up a couple of the Walkers in pretty good shape."

Finn paused and exhaled. "Yup. It was unfortunate. They ran their mouths and wanted to step outside, but I didn't feel like going out."

"Ma said the younger one might have brain damage?"

Sean took a drink off from the jar. "How can they tell? He wasn't that fuckin' bright to start with."

Alston laughed. "None of em' are I guess."

Finn wasn't laughing. "Well, it's over now. I moved on. Hope they have. I was in a bad place, and they picked a bad time."

There was a long silence as the three watched the meat on the fire.

Alston looked at Sean. "Ma said you knocked some girl up?"

Sean's face flushed to a medium red. "Jeez Alston. Just come out and ask I guess."

"Well, did you?"

Sean looked at the ground. "Yeah. I did. Her folks wouldn't let her marry me. I would have you know."

Finn put his hand on Sean's shoulder. "We know. We would have made you."

"Hopefully, you learned your lesson and not be so careless. I don't understand how that could happen." Alston added.

Finn gave Alston a long look. "He doesn't understand Sean. He' still a virgin. Once he does, *it*, he'll know how things could get out of hand."

Alston scowled and poked at the fire. "I'm waiting for marriage. Like in the bible."

Finn laughed. "The bible was written by a bunch of virgins. I can assure you that people fucked before marriage long before the Catholic church laid down its rules."

"Well, I'm waiting, anyway. For a *good* woman."

Sean straightened up. "Doing it before you're married doesn't make anyone bad. Harriett doesn't have a bad bone in her body. I'm not bad. We just had urges and... well... we acted on them. Doesn't mean we're going to hell. Just means we were young."

Finn patted him on the back. "That's right Sean. You tell him."

Alston took the jar from Sean. "Christ, if I would have known you guys would gang up on me. I might have tried to learn to shoot opposite handed and stayed in." He took a drink and grimaced at the harshness of the drink. "Holy cow, that's rugged."

Sean grinned. "I'll get better at it."

Finn took a swig and choked it down. "It would be hard to get worse."

Sean stiffened and took the jar. "Bring your own then."

Finn reached into his back pocket and produced a flask. "I did." He took a sip and handed it to Alston.

Alston took a drink and smiled. "Canadian Whiskey. Good stuff." He handed the flask back to Finn, who put it back in his pocket and walked away.

"You guys are bastards," Sean said, shaking his head.

Alston shrugged. "Enjoy your turpentine." Then followed Finn.

Alston was ten yards away before Sean thought of a response. "It was Pat's deer recipe!"

Alston entered the kitchen to the smells of his childhood. Warm biscuits. Apple pie. The one-of-a-kind smell of a Christmas tree. It made him feel good to be home. He looked around the room and thought how fortunate they were to have each other. Finn looked like a shell of his former self, but he was tough, and he had Mae. Lewin was getting around well without his cane and looked like he'd make close to a full recovery, and he had Cecelia to help him along. Emma and Bill were beaming with their baby, Daniel, and things couldn't be better for them. Even the normally cranky Allison was pleasant, and Melvin doted on her and the boys like they were his own. Young Jim looked a lot like Alston's brother Jim, with his red hair and Alan looked a lot like Calvin. Fortunately, people often remarked that he looked like Melvin too. No one had seen Calvin in months, and everyone was happier for it. Frances and Lillian were the mother hens for the small children, which gave the adults time to visit with each other undistracted.

He was sitting beside the woodstove, enjoying the heat on his skin and admiring his mother. She was the toughest of them all. No matter how bad things might get, she kept the family on the right path. She said that she only wanted one thing for Christmas, and she would never ask for another gift for the rest of her life. "Just bring her boys home safe."

So far three were back. All a little stove up, but they came home alive. Only Alder, Patrick and Joe were still in harm's way and if the war went on much longer, Sean may be joining them soon. The meal was fantastic as usual, and Alston was stuffed. He hadn't eaten like that in more than a year. As they were all about to step onto the porch for a smoke, Finn spoke up.

"Hey everybody. Hold up. I have a surprise."

Everyone stopped and waited. He had a stoic almost melancholy look and Alston thought that this probably wasn't a good surprise.

"Don't tell us you're going back in," quipped Melvin.

Mae laughed. "Huh! No! Not if he wants to stay married."

Finn grinned a little. "No. It's nothing like that. I have a letter from Pat. He sent it to me because he wanted it read when everyone was together."

Alston took off his coat and listened along with everyone else.

"He's fine. He's leaving the submariner service."

Mary smiled and crossed herself. "Thank you, Lord."

"Well hold on. He's not on submarines anymore, but he's not coming home. He's been promoted and is going to train men in anti-sub warfare."

Now everyone was quiet.

"In California."

Alston's heart sunk. He missed his brother so much and now it would be that much longer. "For Christ's sake. Did he say why?"

"He likes being in the Navy. He might make a career of it," Finn said.

Alston was done listening. He put his coat back on, stepped outside, and lit a cigarette. No one came outside for some time to give him some space. But eventually, the door opened, and Mary stepped out. "Have a spare?"

Alston pulled the pack from his coat pocket and handed her the lighter and the pack. "Help yourself Ma."

She lit the cigarette and barely inhaled. "Whew, these are more rugged than I remember."

"Yeah, they do have a burn to em."

"I remember when he got promoted the first time. We had a smoke out here together. Do you remember?"

"Yeah, of course I do," he said and took another drag.

"Well, things haven't changed. He liked it then and he still likes it."

Alston nodded.

"At least he's in the states and you can call him now."

Alston shrugged. "Hell, I could go see him if I wanted to I guess."

"You should. It would be good for you. You could take a train."

Alston stood trying to talk himself out of it, but he couldn't. He had no work yet and really had nothing holding him here at the moment. Then he realized that his money wouldn't last him very long without work. "I can't really afford it now. Maybe after I work for a while."

"You have enough money. You have plenty of money," she said with a grin. She snuffed out the cigarette and tossed the butt into a can. "We never needed any of the money you sent home, so I saved it all. Pat's too. It's a pretty tidy sum. A shade over a thousand dollars."

Alston stood frozen for a moment, trying to let his mind comprehend that sum. Thirty-five dollars a month for thirty months. One thousand and fifty dollars. He had only seen that much money once in his life and that came from his brothers selling illegal whiskey when he was still young.

"Ma. I can't believe it. Why?... How?"

Mary smiled from ear to ear. "I was saving it and then I realized that we didn't need it, so I figured it would be a good nest egg for you to start your lives when you got home."

His mind suddenly realized the possibilities, and he smiled. "I need to see about a train ticket." He squeezed his mother and kissed her cheek. "Thank you, Ma. I love you," he whispered.

"I love you too, son. You're a good man."

Thirty

March 1945

Joyce looked like a miniature version of Daisy with curly blond hair all askew. The March breeze was playing havoc with her tiny curls. She held a sign and stared down the tracks, looking for the first signs of a train.

"Mama? Which way will daddy come from?"

Daisy inhaled and then exhaled in a long, slow breath. "That way, sweetheart. The same way I said the last ten times you asked me. Daddy should be here any minute."

"Mama?"

"Yes."

"I have to pee."

Daisy closed her eyes and calmed herself to prevent exploding. "Of course, you do." Daisy knew well enough that saying, *I have to pee* meant it was imminent. "Okay, let's go... Quickly."

Ruth stepped up and took Joyce's hand. "I'll take her. There's no way I'd let you miss seeing my brother after all this time."

Daisy smiled. "Thank you, Ruth. I appreciate it more than you know."

Ruth hurried Joyce to the restroom and all the McGinns on the platform waited and stared at the northbound track.

"It's coming," said Finn.

"I don't see anything," replied Lewin.

Finn pointed into the sky to a cloud of coal smoke rising above the trees. "There. It's the smoke from the stack. He'll be here soon."

A few seconds later, the train made its turn and was coming to toward the platform.

Mae walked to Daisy and whispered. "It's the greatest feeling of your life. Soak it up."

The engine came by quickly and then started to slow. Daisy could see that the passenger cars were at the rear and she found it hard to fill her lungs. She was so anxious.

"I'm back, mama," called Joyce from behind her.

Daisy turned and positioned her in front, with her welcome home sign.

As the train pulled to a stop, she could see Alder in the window, beaming. She saw him look down at Joyce and burst into laughter. Daisy leaned forward and could see that the sign was upside-down.

He emerged from the train on the steps between the cars and Joyce ran toward him with her curls bouncing wildly behind her.

Alder stepped forward and scooped her up and twirled her around kissing her cheeks over and over.

"Put me down Daddy. I'm dizzy." She protested.

He lowered her gently to the ground and turned to see Daisy in front of him with a brown-haired baby boy on her hip. When he smiled at Edwin who was two now, it was like looking into a tiny mirror. They shared the very same facial features. As he moved closer, Edwin hid his face in Daisy's collar.

"He's shy," she said and tried to get him to look at Alder.

Alder looked at her and thought that she must be the most beautiful woman she had ever seen. She had the face of an angel and the body of a woman. "How about you? You shy?"

"No, I'm not," she said and handed Edwin to Ruth. She turned back to her husband and kissed him. She squeezed him and kissed him some more. It was heaven, somehow she had an overwhelming feeling that everything would be alright now that they were back together. When they finished kissing. The family all stepped in to welcome him home. Mary and each sibling took turns with their welcome and Finn waited to be last.

He stepped up to Alder and looked him over thoroughly. "In one piece I see."

"Should be. I never even fired my weapon. The worst wound I got was barking my knuckles on a Jeep transmission. No medals for me."

Finn scoffed. "Have mine. The things you do to get a medal, don't make it worth it. I assure you."

Alder looked at Finn and could see the sadness in his eyes. "Medals or not. I'm just happy to be with my family."

"It feels good, and once you shake the military routines, it will feel even better. It took me a month to stop wolfing every meal like I might not eat again."

"Miss your rations?"

Finn laughed. "Shit no. I do miss the free cigarettes, though. I swear to God, the cigarette companies put smokes in the rations to get you hooked on their brand when you get out."

Alder laughed. "Might be something to that. I knew a lot of guys who said they didn't smoke, but once live fire started, they all took it up in a hurry."

After they said their welcomes. The whole family headed back to the farm except for Melvin who was headed to the butcher for a couple of corned beef briskets.

He bought the briskets at Joseph's Market. Even though the Morelands sold meats at the store, Joseph's had the best cuts, and their corned beef was legendary. Melvin picked up the briskets and was loading them into the car when he heard his name.

"Melvin!" It was Darby Oates. One of Tom Diamond's men.

"Darby. What's new in the world?"

"Tom wants to see you."

Melvin was curious. "Where is he?"

Darby pointed across Main St. "Across the street at the Woolworth's lunch counter."

Melvin loaded the beefs into the passenger seat and walked across the street. The Woolworth's lunch counter was busy, but Tom held him a seat.

Tom smiled. "Hello Melvin. I thought I saw you drive by. Lunch?"

Melvin shook Tom's hand. "Nah., I have two corned beef briskets in the car. Alder McGinn came home today. So, we're having a big shindig out to the farm."

"Well, shit I won't keep you then. Have you seen your brother, Calvin?"

"Not for a couple of years. Why?"

Tom grinned. "He's in town and rumor has it he's flushed with cash."

Melvin shook his head. *What an idiot*, he thought. But then he suddenly felt angry. He has cash to play the big man, but doesn't try to do anything for his sons. "He's not worth my time."

Tom took a sip of coffee. "He's worth mine."

Suddenly Melvin realized that Tom was asking if Melvin minded if they recovered the swindled funds from his brother. At first, he had the inclination to protect Calvin, but then remembered their last conversation and his warning for Cal to stay away. "Do what you need to do, Tom. He's a big boy. Let him take his medicine."

Tom smiled from ear to ear. "I knew you'd say that. If we get any money, I'll send you half."

"I don't want his money." Melvin said with a frown.

"I know you don't. But be sure those boys get it. You might start a savings account for each of them. Could help em' to buy a house someday."

Melvin could see the logic in that. They wouldn't miss it if it was already in the bank. "Fair enough. I'll do that." They shook hands again and Melvin looked at Tom. "I don't want to know what happens to him. I'll remember him from back when we were kids."

Tom grinned like big cat. "I'm just looking to collect what was stole. The rest is up to him."

That evening Melvin was in the barn drinking coffee while the McGinns passed a bottle of whiskey around. They stood next to a small fire, laughing and talking. It was one of the things Melvin missed the most after the others all went to war. Just talking like men.

As they talked, a pair of headlights turned in to the driveway.

Everyone looked up to see the silhouette of a man in the glare of the headlights.

"Who the hell is this?" asked Finn.

The man walked forward and called out, "I'm looking for Melvin Carrigan!"

Melvin looked confused. He wasn't expecting company. "Can I help you?"

"Tom said to drop this off. He said it's a gift." It was Darby again.

"Oh, hey Darby, what's this about a gift?" asked Melvin.

Darby shrugged. "No idea. He just told me to bring this out here and to say welcome home to Alder."

Alder was surprised and had no idea who had sent the message. "Thanks?"

Darby handed Melvin a small box tied with a string.

Melvin looked it over. "Thanks, Darby."

Oates waved and returned to his car, then headed back toward town.

Melvin brought the box to the barn and untied the string.

"What's in it?" asked Sean.

"How the hell would he know that?" asked Finn. "Christ, you're dense."

Melvin peeled back the lid and saw a ring, some cash, and a note. He pulled the ring and money from the box and opened the note. It was then that he saw the bloody teeth laying in the bottom of the box. Four long teeth that looked suspiciously like a man's front top teeth. Melvin shook his head and passed the box. Then read the note aloud.

"Mel. Here's his wedding band. He doesn't want it anymore. Forty dollars for his boys and four teeth so that he won't have anything to lie through anymore. He's paid in full now. Tom"

"What's all this?" asked Alder.

Melvin folded the note and tossed it into the fire. "Hopefully, the last we'll see of my brother. He was warned to stay away, but the man has no sense." He took the box back and tossed it in as well. Somehow, he remembered that teeth and bone don't burn, so he threw another piece of wood on top of the box so that he would never see those teeth again.

Two of Tom Diamond's men dragged Calvin to the far end of the rail yard where two hobos were cooking a soup on a fire. They dropped Cal next to the fire.

The larger man stepped up. "How would you like to make five dollars each?"

The hobos looked at Calvin and each other. One looked up from where he was seated. "Do we have to kill him?"

The big man laughed. "Ha-ha. No, just the opposite. Get him on a train and get him south of here. Way south. New Hampshire or Massachusetts preferably."

The men looked at each other and nodded. "Deal."

The big man pulled a wad of ones from his pocket and counted out ten bills and handed them each five. Before he put his money away, he tossed a one on Calvin's chest. "To feed him."

"We'll feed him, mister."

"Good." The two men started to walk away when the big one stopped and turned. "Oh yeah, and if you're thinking about taking the money and running, the next time someone finds you, you'll be in worse shape than him. I promise."

The lead hobo nodded. "He'll get there. We'll keep our word."

"Thank you."

Thirty–One

May 7, 1945

The breakfast rush was winding down in the Moreland Diner. Men were coming home, and even though the war was still going on, life seemed to have a little more normalcy with the return of familiar faces. Everyone with a job was off to work, and only the regulars remained.

Mortimer Miles was a retired lawyer and spent his mornings reading the paper and drinking coffee after coffee for the price of a cup. He occasionally ordered breakfast, but generally it was toast and coffee. Nothing else. On top of that, he never left a tip. He wasn't one of Ruth's favorites. He tended to be arrogant, and most people found him exceedingly condescending. The diner patrons tended to be country people that worked hard and didn't have a lot of schooling.

Emmett Hilton was another regular, but he was always kind and often tried to leave a tip. Ruth knew his family. She had gone to school with his girls and refused to accept it. Emmett's wife had died, and he had never remarried. He came to the diner to get away from the farm and avoid having to cook for himself. Sometimes if he came in for dinner, she would buy him a slice of pie and tell him that it was going to get thrown out, so he should eat it, to avoid making it look like charity.

The two couldn't have been more different. Miles was bald, with squinty blue eyes and a beak of a nose. He wore glasses that hung low, and he had a habit of looking at you over them, which made him look all the more condescending. He never smiled.

Emmett had a full head of hair, and in spite of being in his late sixties, he had hardly any grays. His hair was still dark somewhere between black and brown. He had kind brown eyes like a dog, and he always smiled.

Emmett glanced over at Miles and his paper. "War in Europe will be over soon, eh Mort?"

Miles lowered the paper and looked at Emmett and sighed. "I doubt that, Emmett. This is likely to drag on for months. Hitler may be dead, but the Germans are fighting for their homeland."

Emmett shrugged. "We got a lot of boys over there. Tough boys. I think they'll whoop the Germans in good shape."

Miles put down his paper. "Would you care to wager? I'll bet you one dollar that the Germans won't quit until at least the 4th of July?"

"Oh, I don't bet money. Worked too hard for it."

Miles snickered and picked up his paper. "Your loss, I guess. Mark my words. This isn't ending anytime soon."

Ruth refilled Emmett's coffee and leaned in toward him to whisper. "I hope it ends soon, too. I miss my Joe."

Ruth started rolling silverware into napkins in preparation for lunch. She found herself lost in a daydream, thinking of Joe. The radio small radio in the corner of the diner was playing the hits of the day. She found herself suddenly melancholy when she heard the piano opening of *I'll be seeing you* came on. She loved that song. It reminded her of Joe, and she felt it in her heart. It was the Billie Holiday version, which was her favorite. A lot of people liked the Sinatra version better, but she felt like Billie was singing from a woman's point of view. To Ruth, it was the only point of view that made sense. All the women were waiting at home. Waiting and praying that their men would come back. Back into their arms. Oh, how she'd hold him. She had thought about his homecoming every day since he left. She just wanted to leap into his arms and stay there for a day. Maybe two. It made her start to well up just thinking about it.

Midway through the song, the radio station interrupted. At first Ruth was angry. The stupid radio announcer had broken her bliss.

"We interrupt this program to bring you a broadcast from the President."

"Turn it up!" shouted a man in the corner.

Ruth walked to the radio and turned it up. The radio crackled and snapped. Then she heard President Truman start to speak.

"This is a solemn but a glorious hour. I only wish that Franklin D. Roosevelt had lived to witness this day. General

Eisenhower informs me that the forces of Germany have surrendered to the United Nations. The flags of freedom fly over all Europe."

The diner exploded in a cry of human emotion that made Ruth freeze and stop breathing. A moment later, she gasped, and the tears began to pour from her eyes.

"Listen!" someone yelled, and the room went quiet.

"For this victory, we join in offering our thanks to the Providence which has guided and sustained us through the dark days of adversity." He paused for a moment.

"Our rejoicing is sobered and subdued by a supreme consciousness of the terrible price we have paid to rid the world of Hitler and his evil band. Let us not forget, my fellow Americans, the sorrow and the heartache which today abide in the homes of so many of our neighbors-neighbors whose most priceless possession has been rendered as a sacrifice to redeem our liberty."

She immediately thought of her mother-in-law Nora and Johnny. The loss had seemed to crush Nora's spirit for a time. It was like her mother when Jim died. Day after day without a smile. It was like a part of her soul died with Jim. She was sure it was the same with Nora.

The door to the Diner burst open and Earl Merrill entered ready for action. "What happened?! I heard the screaming. Is everything alright?" The first face he saw was Ruth's, and it was red, and tears were streaming down her face.

"It's alright Earl. Germany surrendered." She said and smiled.

Earl balled his right hand into a fist and shook it in excitement. "Thank you, lord!" he cried and ran out the door toward the store. Bill and Emma saw him running and stepped outside.

"Germany surrendered! Germany surrendered!" He yelled. Bill and Emma stood in momentary confusion as the words finally sunk in.

"Are you sure?" Bill asked.

"It's on the radio! I could hear the President!"

Bill grabbed Emma and squeezed her kissing her over and over. "Only Japan left now!"

Joe low-crawled though, the jungle vegetation. The ground was slick and stunk of wet, rotting leaves. The sound of bullets was coming from in front of him and behind him. His OSS Operational group had been assigned to Operation Blueberry, training Chinese soldiers as commandos in Burma and they were tasked with pushing the Japanese off the road that connected Burma to China.

"Roy!" he heard a voice call out. It was his Captain, Jim Cook. "Can you make the pillbox?"

Joe peeked through the plants to see the opening of the fortification. It was smokey from the machine gun fire and seemed to be a continuous flicker of muzzle flashes. He looked for a landmark to judge the distance. *Home to second*, he thought. Just like Yogi Berra.

"I can make it Cap!" he yelled back. His heart was pounding through his chest.

"On three make the throw. We'll cover you! Got it?!"

Joe pulled a grenade from his belt and squatted as low as possible to still be able to spring up. He slid his right finger into the ring and squeezed the grenade with his left. He took a deep breath. *Runner is stealing second*, he thought.

"Got it!"

"One! Two! Three!"

On three, Joe sprang up like a catcher out of a crouch out of the jungle and his arm snapped off a laser of a throw. He saw the grenade leave his hand, and then he saw the sniper. The whole moment felt like it was frozen in time. He saw the muzzle flash and simultaneously he saw a hole appear in the sniper's forehead. The man fell and Joe thought that maybe the weapon had misfired. That was until he felt his left shoulder scream in pain and the force of being knocked backward.

He was hit, but he still couldn't comprehend what had happened. The impact had knocked the wind out of him and he fought to expand his lungs. For a moment, he felt panicked and then his body let him breathe.

He gasped, and then they were working again.

"Medic!" he heard someone shout. Then his friend Jim Gardelle dragged him further back down the slope he had just crawled up.

Doc Johnson arrived a few seconds later and continued dragging him as Gardelle headed for the pillbox with the rest of the team, blasting away.

"I'm hit doc." Joe said. "Is it bad?"

Johnson looked at the wound. "Straight through."

Johnson quickly cut his shirt away and placed bandages on the entry and exit wounds. He felt the collar bone and saw the wound was below it. He rolled him to his right side and felt for the scapula. The exit missed that as well.

"Million dollar wound, Joe. Nothing vital hit. But I dare say you won't be making that throw again anytime soon. God must love you."

Joe chuckled, and that shot a bolt of pain into his shoulder. "Ow!" he said and pressed on the bandage with a grimace. "He does love me."

The firing continued for another couple of minutes, and Joe heard a series of loud pops as three or four grenades went off within seconds of each other.

"Medic!" they could hear being yelled from up the slope.

"Gotta go, Joe!" he said and grabbed his medic kit. "You'll be fine. Rest easy." Then he was gone.

Joe was left-handed and tried to shift his Thompson to his right. He could still use his arm. It was just excruciating to lift it. He propped up against a tree and moved his left arm to give him something to rest the gun on. He lowered the butt end to raise the elevation of the barrel. He couldn't see above the plants, but the firing had ended, and he heard men speaking English.

"Joe! Where are you?" It was Gardelle.

"Here!" Joe yelled back and Jim emerged through the plants.

Jim flopped down beside him and tried to catch his breath. "You hit bad?"

"Doc says straight through."

Jim pulled a cigarette from a pack in his pocket and lit it. "You are one lucky SOB." He took a drag and exhaled a big cloud of smoke up into the air. "Captain Cook saved your backside with that shot."

Joe was confused. "What shot?"

"Head hot. The sniper. He put a round in the guy's forehead just as he was pulling the trigger. That's probably how he hit your shoulder instead of your heart."

Joe nodded and winced in pain. "So that's what happened? I thought maybe his weapon misfired."

Jim exhaled another cloud of smoke and chuckled. "He's a hell of a shot. That's for sure. He popped up and pow. Right between the lookers. He had to find the target, aim and fire in about a second."

"I already knew where he was," said a voice in the bushes, and Captain Cook pushed aside the leaves and stepped into the little clearing where Joe was sitting. "I saw his muzzle flash a couple of times and figured I'd try for him first. You hit bad Joe?"

"Doc doesn't think so."

"That was a hell of a throw. It was a dart right between the two guns. As soon as it went off, I knew we had that box."

"Thanks Captain." Joe smiled. "And thanks for that shot. My wife appreciates it, I assure you."

Thirty-Two

September 2, 1945

The sun shone through the cabin window and woke up Ruth. It was Sunday, and it was the first night they had spent together away from their home since their honeymoon. It was simple, but felt magical at the same time. They were only a couple of miles from home, but it felt like a world away. She woke up in Joe's arms and laid there for a while enjoying the feeling of his chest rising and falling against her back. When she was fully awake, she slid out from under him and rolled over and watched him sleep. She felt tears start to well in her eyes as she watched. She didn't know why except she loved him so much and now he was home.

She looked at the scar on the front of his left shoulder where the bullet had torn through his body. It was red and still swollen. Someday it would fade away, but it looked so raw it hurt her heart to even see it. As she studied the contours of his chest, she realized the difference between life and death in war was mere inches. There was less than a foot between his scar and the center of his chest.

When Joe got home. The first place he went after visiting his folks and the farm was the cemetery on the outskirts of town. It was a simple headstone. John's body was buried on the other side of the world. Finn had collected his possessions and sent them home, but John was gone, and Joe felt like a piece of him was lost as well. Finn had said that he was only hit once. Straight through the heart. It kept his family from imagining the truth that he was hit many times. In their minds, it was cleaner this way.

Everyone was home now. Joe was the last one back. He had been home a little over two weeks. They patched his shoulder up and sent him to a convalescence hospital in Virginia, and when he healed, and then discharged. It was surprising, because the Japanese hadn't surrendered yet and Joe knew they were tough and likely to fight to the last man.

It was nearly nine o'clock in the morning and she knew Joe would be upset to miss mass. He was a devout Catholic, and he loved the church. He told Ruth he had been to confession several times since leaving Burma. Not because he was sinning, but because he struggled to reconcile the killings in his heart. In his mind, he knew he was doing his duty, but in his heart he felt that he had offended God and maybe he wouldn't go to heaven.

"Joe," she whispered.

He didn't move. He was in a deep sleep.

"Joe," she whispered again and lightly shook him.

This time he heard her, and his mouth formed into a grin. Then he opened his sleepy eyes.

"Have I died and gone to heaven? I think I see an angel."

Ruth laughed and shoved him. "We'll be late for church while you lay about in bed."

He reached out and snatched Ruth, pulling her to him. He kissed her and squeezed her tight.

Between kisses, she pulled back. "Joe. We'll be late for mass."

Joe looked at her slid her hand down to under the sheets. "God will understand."

They missed mass and at first Ruth felt guilty, but then she thought about it some more. *I waited all that time and he talked with God more than me. It's my turn.*

The farm was buzzing with excitement. Sean cooked four chickens and a leg of lamb on a spit in the front yard. As soon as Ruth and Joe stepped from the car, the smell made their stomachs rumble. The aroma of hot meat in the air smelled like heaven to Joe. He always appreciated his army meals, but rarely enjoyed them. Everything was salty. Saltier than a typical person could usually tolerate, and that made him thirstier. The mere thought of roasted chicken made his mouth water.

"Joe," called Sean. "Would you like a bit of crispy skin?

Joe lit up. He couldn't remember the last time he had a chicken that wasn't boiled. Just the thought of crispy skin was the greatest thing he could think of at that moment. It was funny how the little things seemed to take on much greater meaning when you are deprived of everything.

Sean pulled a long knife from a box near the spit and cut Joe a crispy piece of skin from where the neck would have been. "It's hot."

Joe took the morsel and blew on it a couple of times. The smell of fried chicken skin made him even hungrier. He put the slab of roasted skin in his mouth and the crunch made him so happy that it was hard to comprehend how something so trivial could bring so much satisfaction.

Alder opened window and moved the radio to the sill. "Listen to this!" he yelled and turned the radio up as loud as it would go. Everyone stood in place, listening intently to the broadcast.

My fellow Americans, and the Supreme Allied Commander, General MacArthur, in Tokyo Bay:

The thoughts and hopes of all America–indeed of all the civilized world–are centered tonight on the battleship Missouri. There on that small piece of American soil anchored in Tokyo Harbor the Japanese have just officially laid down their arms. They have signed terms of unconditional surrender.

Four years ago, the thoughts and fears of the whole civilized world were centered on another piece of American soil–Pearl

Harbor. The mighty threat to civilization which began there is now laid at rest. It was a long road to Tokyo–and a bloody one.

We shall not forget Pearl Harbor.

The Japanese militarists will not forget the U.S.S. Missouri.

"God damn right." Finn said and took a sip from a flask. He put the stopper on it and handed it to Mae. "It's over."

He looked at Joe and Ruth standing together and thought about John Roy. He missed him.

He looked at Alder and Lewin with their families and realized that was how it was supposed to be. He didn't begrudge them not seeing actual combat. It was unnatural and evil. He wasn't sure how many men he had killed, and the burden seemed to weigh down his very soul. They all came home intact. No, neatly folded flags in place of a son. They were all safe now.

Mary stepped onto the porch and wiped her hands on her apron. She looked at each son with sincere reverence. "Your Da would have been proud of you boys. You did your duty, and you came home safely. It's all he ever cared about." She paused for a moment and fought back some tears. "There's no duty greater than family," she paused again. "He was... right," she said and started to sob.

As they all tried to comfort her, the moment was broken by the sound of a car pulling into the driveway. The family all stopped and stared at the stranger as he got out of the vehicle.

"I'm looking for the McGinn farm," said Freddie who seemed a little confused about what was going on.

Finn turned and smiled. "Frances!"

Frances stepped forward. She had a crinkled brow and curly red hair. She squinted a little as the sunset half blinded her. "Yes?"

Finn stepped forward and hugged Freddie. Then turned and put his arm around him. "There's someone I'd like you to meet."

EPILOGUE

July 5, 2008

Finn sat in a chair at Maple Ridge nursing home in Monroe. They had dressed him in his finest suit. In fact, his only suit. He was the last of the twelve. Today Lillian was being buried and he would be alone.

It wasn't supposed to be like this. He was the second oldest and had just turned ninety-six, he felt like he should have died a long time ago. But he just wouldn't die.

Sean had died in 1952 in the Korean war and was the only one to actually die in combat. He had never married, and his only child Daniel was raised by Emma and Bill.

Mary McGinn, the rock of the family, died in the early morning hours of November 22nd, 1963. Later that day, President Kennedy was shot. Finn always said that two great people died that day.

Bill Moreland passed in 1966 from a heart attack, which was a shame because he was still a young man. Emma continued making dresses until she closed her shop in 1984. She had and never remarried and died in her sleep in 1999. Their son Daniel and his sons still run the Moreland operations around the county.

Lewin died from bone cancer in 1979. By the time he passed, he was nothing more than a skeleton with skin. Cecelia could carry him around the house in spite of him being well over a foot taller than her. She had been a resident at Maple Ridge too until her death in 2000. They ate meals together and laughed about the old days. She was a terrible card player, but Finn was happy for the companionship.

Alder and Daisy both died of natural causes in the nineteen-eighties, as did Ruth. Joe lived until 1997, but he had developed dementia so severely that he didn't ever remember ever serving in the OSS.

Finn's soulmate Mae passed in 1991, and he never remarried. She was the most loving and patient woman in the world, and he missed her terribly.

Allison and Melvin were eventually married, and she died in 1995 a year after Melvin. As often happens, people forget the truth and most folks believed that Melvin had always been her husband. No one could recall what Calvin even looked like. Calvin had drank and smoked himself to death in 1990. He had been in and out of the boys lives, usually to try to borrow money.

Patrick ended his days in California in June 1994 and true to form Alston died eleven months later in May 1995. They had stayed in Marin County, California their whole adult lives. After the war, they both worked at Mare Island and had a hand in the building of twenty-one submarines and the repair of dozens of others.

Frances and Freddie Dumond went on to have eight children. The most of any of the McGinn children. One boy, then seven girls. That poor bastard. Finn had always been close to Freddie, and it hurt him terribly when cancer took him in the early nineties. Frances lived until December 2001 when she died from pneumonia.

Lillian visited him regularly until her death last week, and now it was him alone. She married but never had children. There was something about growing up in such a large family that kept most of them from having large families of their own.

They were all gone now. All but him.

Finn thought about wheeling himself out into the hallway to watch the *goings ons*, but he was too damned tired to push that chair.

He heard a knock at his door, and he turned to see Jim and Alan. That made him smile. Jim reminded him of his brother Jim, or at least how he remembered him. It had been sixty-nine years since Jim had died. It didn't seem possible that it could be that long.

"Take me outside." He said somewhat gruffly.

"The funeral is not for a couple of hours yet," said Jim.

Finn frowned. "I didn't ask for an itinerary. I just want to go outside."

"Okay, fair enough," said Alan and pushed the chair out into the sun. "Where to?"

Finn looked around. "Over there behind those huge lilacs, so I can get some shade."

"Or so that they can't see you?" asked Jim.

"Huh. That's a matter of perspective," Finn grumbled. When they reached the shade, it was quite pleasant. Finn looked at each of them. "Smokes?"

"We quit," said Jim and Alan nodded.

"You candy assed sons-o-bitches," he said with a scowl.

Jim smiled and produced a corncob pipe from his pocket and packed it with tobacco. He handed it to Finn and helped him to light it. Finn grinned through toothless gums and blew a puff of smoke in the air. "You pull that stunt with the whiskey and we're gonna' have a go."

Alan produced a large flask and paper cups. He poured them each a drink and put the flask back in his pocket.

Jim held up his cup. "To aunt Lil."

"Lil" repeated Alan and Finn just nodded, and they all drank.

Finn held out his cup again and Alan refilled it. Finn drank it down and held it out again.

Alan hesitated and looked at Jim.

"Don't look at him. Just pour," barked Finn.

Alan refilled the cup and Finn drank it, then crushed the cup. He puffed on the pipe and a tear was running down his cheek.

He wiped it away and handed the pipe to Jim. "Take me back inside, boys."

"We can go to the funeral now and visit if you want," said Alan.

Finn shook his head no. "I'm not going. I'm going to bed. I'm so damned tired."

Alan was about to protest when Jim stopped him short. "Sure, thing Uncle Finn."

They brought him back to his room and sat him in his sitting chair.

Finn looked at them and smiled. "Don't come back here anymore."

"What?" asked Jim.

"Remember me like we just were a few minutes ago. Or like how I was when you were kids. Not a broken-down old man."

"But..."

Fin held up a hand. "I'm tired boys. Time to go. Send my love to everyone there."

"Okay do you need anything else before we go?"

"Yes. Leave the flask. You can pick it up later."

Alan looked at Jim, and Jim shrugged. So, Alan handed over the flask and the two men kissed him on the cheek, gave him a hug and left.

Finn rinsed his dentures in mouthwash to hide the liquor smell, and after his evening meds, he sat up in bed and pulled the flask from his drawer. He drank and thought about his family. When the flask was empty, he shut out the light and closed his eyes. His heart was pounding now from the combination of medication and whiskey. As he drifted off, he saw Mae and Mary walking toward him. He called to them, and they walked closer. Mae looked as beautiful as the first day he had seen her in the hospital.

She reached out and pulled him to her, then kissed him on his lips. "We've been waiting for you."

He looked at Mary and she was younger like when they were kids. She smiled and said, "Welcome home, son."

Afterword

Where do we go from here?

I don't expect to carry this storyline any farther into their future, but I would like to take a look back. Feedback from different readers has inspired me to go back before the Red Road and follow Alvin's journey from Ireland to Maine and the relationship between Alvin and Mary's family.

We have started developing The Red Road as a limited series with the potential for the other books to be future seasons. One character who intrigued the producers was Parker Moreland and other readers have wondered how the two Moreland brothers (Parker and William) became so opposite from one and other. So, they will likely be getting a book or two as well.

So, the saga is far from finished and I look forward to bringing you more tales from Monroe, Maine.

Thank you for your ongoing support.

Jon